All The Way Home

OTHER BOOKS BY RAYNETTA MANEES

All For Love (Book 1 of the SuperStar Series)

All For Love: The SuperStar (Book 2 of the SuperStar Series)

Fantasy

Follow Your Heart

Wishing On A Star

Heart Of The Matter

My Alzheimer's Diary (non-fiction)

[All The Way Home is a novella originally published in the "A Mother's Touch" Anthology. It is now available in this stand-alone edition.]

All The Way Home

By

Raynetta Manees

Print ISBN: 978-1-7321342-2-5
eBook ISBN: 978-0-955324-0-6

Please visit www.RManees.com for additional author information and appearance dates.

Dedication

This book is dedicated to my granddaughter, Zayna Raylon Hurd, for some quotes I never would have thought of on my own!

And to my grandmother, Annie McDonald Knight, who turned 100 in the month this book was originally released

Acknowledgment

To my good friend, Dr. LaSalles Pinnock.   Thank you for being such a special godfather to my child.

CHAPTER 1

"Mr. Jamison?   Mr. Jamison!"   After a man shouldering a two-by-four pointed him out for her Jolene had to sprint to catch up with Jamison's rapidly retreating broad back.

Jamison turned to glance at her briefly.   "Yes?" a deep and somewhat irritated voice replied as he continued on his way.

"Mr. Jamison..."   By then they had reached gravel. One of Jolene's high heels caught on a rock, and she stumbled.   She threw her arms outward, just barely regaining her balance before falling.   Mr. Broad Back stopped then, turned, and crouched to pick up the notepad and pen she had dropped.

"Are you all right?" he asked, handing back her things. He seemed grudgingly concerned, despite his full lips being drawn into a severe straight line.

Jolene couldn't help but think how handsome his face would have been had it been cordial.   However, he seemed anything *but* cordial. "Yes.   Yes, I'm fine," Jolene gasped, as off-handedly as she could manage.   Truth to tell, she had turned her ankle and had begun to feel a small but very definite throb.   But Jolene was danged if she'd let *him* know that.   *Who does he think he is, anyway, turning his back on me and walking away like that?*

Jamison merely grunted in reply.   *Jeez, what a charmer,* Jolene mused on.   *Just a massive—albeit fine— hunk of muscle with no couth, and no class.*

"Mr. Jamison, I'm Jolene Jefferies from Channel Seven, and..."

"I know who you are," he said shortly, starting once again toward the rear of the site.   "You were *supposed* to be here two hours ago."

"Yes. I know. I'm sorry." Jolene was losing in her struggle to keep up with him, the ankle aching more and more with each step. "But there was a fire downtown we had to cover, and..." *Why am I explaining myself to this...this Neanderthal?* Jolene suddenly reflected. She stopped abruptly. Jamison went several paces before he realized she was no longer beside him and stopped.

"What's the matter?" he queried.

"Nothing. Nothing at all, Mr. Jamison," Jolene replied in her best nice-nasty tone, looking him dead in his charcoal black eyes. "It's just that I'm getting the impression this is not a particularly expedient time for your interview."

Jamison crossed his arms. "Two hours ago would have been a lot more expedient," he pithily replied.

"Hey, Ronny!" a man yelled from the back of the lot. "You think this cement is gonna wait 'til you *feel* like pouring it? And you know we've only got the mixer until six o'clock!"

"And that's *why* two hours ago would have been more expedient," Jamison continued, sweeping his arm toward the guy. "I'm trying to *construct* something right now, lady. That's what a construction company does. And I ain't got time now for styling and profiling on TV!"

The nerve of him! "I see," Jolene came back frostily. "Perhaps we can set another date for your interview next week—*if* we can fit it into *our* schedule!" She turned curtly to her cameraman. "Come on, Frank. Let's get out of here, and let Mr. Jamison get on with his *constructing*!"

But Jolene's turn was a bit *too* curt. The injured ankle suddenly gave, and this time she couldn't recover her footing. Frank reached for her, but the camera was in his way. Jolene braced herself for the bruising punishment of the gravel but instead found herself suddenly lifted up. Jamison had bridged the few feet between them in seconds and effortlessly swept Jolene up into his powerful arms.

Jamison looked down at Jolene, "Maybe *next week* it'll occur to you to not wear high heels to a construction site..." Wonder of wonders—a smile slowly materialized over his comely features, "...not even ones as cute as these," he continued, glancing at Jolene's feet.

Jolene was speechless—and only partially from the suddenness of the situation.

Jamison turned his head and was staring deeply into her eyes, as though he was really seeing her for the first time. Jolene found herself momentarily transfixed by his gaze, by the secure strength of his grasp.   She noticed for the first time the silver strands liberally distributed throughout his thick, curly black hair, and through the lushness of his mustache.   The deep cleft of his chin became more pronounced in accompaniment to the unexpected smile.

"I'm...I'm all right now.   Please put me down," Jolene shakily insisted.   She was mortified.   *Mercy!   He must be strong to pick* me *up like that!   I bet his back is regretting that move right about now.*

"Are you sure?" Jamison asked, with a broad smile.

Why he's laughing *at me!* Jolene's thoughts rushed on. "Yes! Yes, I'm fine."   She said forcefully, squirming in his embrace.   "Put me down!"

Jamison did, reluctantly.   The ankle hurt worse than ever but bore her weight.

"I'm sorry.   But I didn't want you to fall," Jamison's smile grew even wider.   "We're operating on a shoe-string. The last thing we need is a hefty lawsuit from your station," he teased.

"You needn't have worried," Jolene shot back, not seeing much humor in the situation.   She reached up to secure some hairpins that had come loose, allowing a large section of her luxuriant upswept mane to collapse to her shoulders.

"I can take care of myself."

"Yeah.   I sorta picked up on that already," Jamison remarked with an insightful smile.

"O-Hi-O!"   the guy to the rear called out again, apparently still addressing Jamison.   "You comin' or what?"

"Your crew needs you," Jolene primly observed.   She turned away, the ever faithful Frank close behind.

"Hey!   What about next week?" Jamison called after her.

"I'll have my people call your people," Jolene threw over her shoulder as she limped off with as much dignity as she could muster.   She didn't want to look back, but like Lot's wife, couldn't resist.   He was still standing at the same spot, thoughtfully watching her.   The sight of him watching her retreating backside made Jolene strangely self-conscious, but she continued her somewhat unsteady but determined exit.

Jolene looked down at the Ace bandage swaddling her ankle.   *Well, the Bible says pride cometh before a fall,* she thought ruefully.   *Much as I hate to admit it, he was right. I should have known better than to go to a construction site in heels. But I had left my flats at the station, and we were already late, as Hulk Hogan Jamison so emphatically pointed out.*

Jolene sighed.   *Good Lord, that man was fine!   Just my luck to meet him that way.*   She chuckled softly to herself. *As if it would have made a difference if we had met under better circumstances.   He probably has an adoring size nine wife and a house full of babies.*   No—even in their brief and frenzied encounter, Jolene had noticed he wasn't wearing a wedding band.

Then he probably has a string of willowy females only

too ready, willing, and able to satisfy his every whim, she pondered on. Still, somehow she hadn't been able to shake him from her mind.

"Gee-Gee?" a small voice called from inside the house, behind her. Jolene smiled as she heard the quick, tiny footsteps, going first into the master bedroom, and then into the bathroom, in search of her. "Gee-Gee?"

"I'm outside, honey," Jolene called through the patio screen.

The footsteps became a scamper, and Zayna appeared at the patio doors. "What you doing outside, Gee-Gee?"

"Just having my morning coffee, baby. It's such a beautiful morning I thought I'd have it out here." Jolene knew what was coming next.

Sure enough, the determined little voice maintained, "Well, I wanna come out there, too."

"Okay, dear. You can come out. But you have to go put on some shoes and a sweater, and..."

Before she could finish, Zayna was off like a shot, running to her room for the required items that were her passport to the great outdoors.

Jolene had to smile tenderly. *That kid is a pistol. She has so much energy I get tired just watching her.*

In no time flat Zayna was back. Jolene reflected a moment on the items that had no doubt been thrown to the floor of Zayna's closet in her rush to snatch a sweater from a hanger she couldn't yet reach. Zayna came bouncing out the patio doors, to Jolene's surprise actually stopping to slide the screen door closed behind her.

"Thank you for closing the screen, Zayna," Jolene smiled, hoping her recognition of the feat would further reinforce it in the child's mind. After all, girlfriend usually left the door wide open.

Zayna just flashed Jolene a smile and then ran hell-for-leather for her swing set.   Jolene almost laughed aloud at her choice of attire.   Over her purple Barney nightgown, the child had donned not a sweater, but her bright yellow Tweety-Bird raincoat, complete with hood.   On her feet were a pair of hot pink Nikes.   *She's certainly an Equal Opportunity kid,* Jolene assessed with amusement.   *She's giving every color in the rainbow a shot with* that *outfit.*

But having reached the swing, Zayna stopped short. "Gee-Gee!   The birds pee-peed on my swing!"

Jolene was seriously puzzled.   "Uh...What?"

Zayna pointed accusingly to the swing.   "My swing is wet!"   She looked around the spacious yard, peering up into its numerous trees at the birds twittering merrily about. "Those birds pee-peed on my swing!"

What is *this child talking about?* Jolene wondered. Then it dawned on her.   She had to laugh, "Oh, honey. That's not pee-pee.   That's dew.   That's morning dew.   It's on the grass, too, see?"

"Doo?" Zayna echoed skeptically.   "What is doo?"

Okay, Jolene pondered, *how do I explain the concept of "dew" to a four-year-old who doesn't have the word "condensation" in her vocabulary?*   After reflecting another moment, Jolene replied, "Well, baby, once the sun goes down, the air gets cooler at night, right?"

Zayna nodded.   Yes, she knew that part.

"After a while, the ground and things on it are warmer than the air around them.   The water in the air likes warm surfaces, so it settles on them."

Zayna thought about that one a moment.   "So it's like rain?"

"Yes," Jolene agreed, relieved her explanation had not been too complex for the child to grasp.   "Yes, it's similar to the reason it rains."

Zayna nodded again.   Rain she knew about.   If this

stuff was like rain, it wasn't something gross and disgusting. "But my swing is still wet," she pointed out meaningfully.

"We can fix that in a hurry," Jolene replied.   She had brought out a roll of paper towels, to wipe off the patio table and chairs.   She grabbed it and limped carefully over to the swing set.

"Your leg still hurt, Gee-Gee?" Zayna asked with troubled eyes.

"It's not my leg, dear.   It's my ankle.   Do you know what an ankle is?   Show me your ankle," Jolene quizzed as she wiped off the swing.

Zayna grinned proudly as she triumphantly pointed to her own ankle.

"That's right!" Jolene commended her.   "I hurt my ankle yesterday, and I'm staying home from work today, to give it a chance to get better."

Zayna bent over, giving Jolene's ankle close scrutiny. "Did it blood?" she asked earnestly.   Lately, for some ungodly reason, Zayna had been fascinated with the process of bleeding.

"That's 'bleed,' Zee," Jolene patiently explained.   "No, it didn't bleed.   It's hurt inside, where you can't see it."

"But I *can* see it," Zayna disputed, jumping into the swing, after checking to make sure its dryness quotient was to her satisfaction.   "See?" she pointed to Jolene's ankle. "It's big!"

You mean 'bigger,' my love, Jolene thought ruefully. *There's not much tiny on your size 18 'Gee-Gee,' ankles included.*

"That's called 'swollen,' Zayna," Jolene continued aloud. "But it should be better tomorrow.   So today I'm going to stay home with you."

"I'm not going to school?" the child asked, pumping ever higher in the swing.   Zayna called her day-care center 'school,' which Jolene thought was appropriate, since the center had taught Zayna to count to ten in Spanish, and sing the alphabet in Hebrew.

"No, I thought today I'd keep you home with me—unless you *want* me to take you to school."

Zayna pondered this a moment.   She loved school. "No," she finally decided. "I'll stay with you."

Holding on to the side of the swing set for balance, Jolene bowed deeply from the waist at the honor bestowed upon her. "Well, thank you too much, Your Royal Tinyness," she teased.

Zayna just giggled, continuing her soaring reach for the sky, as Jolene painfully made her way back to the patio table and her coffee.   As she reached her chair, Jolene noticed the geraniums in the large stone pots near the rear of the patio.   They were so close to the house that rain barely reached them.   Jolene had, as usual, been so busy she had forgotten to water them.   They looked it.   The gorgeous blooms were starting to wilt.

"Oh, no, you don't," Jolene scolded the flowers.   "I worked too hard planting you to let you die on me.   You get water, stat!"   She picked up the plastic pail she kept near the flowers for just that purpose and set it under the nearby spigot.   When the pail was full, Jolene bent to grab the handle, but since she was already favoring the injured ankle, the added weight upset her symmetry even more.   She wobbled, sloshing water from the heavy pail onto her slippers.

"Whoa!   Better let me get that!"

Hearing an unexpected voice from so close behind her, Jolene dropped the pail entirely.   It hit the concrete patio with a loud *blam*, tipping over and spilling the water down the patio and onto the grass.   Jolene whirled, grabbing a nearby patio chair for balance.

"I'm sorry.   I didn't mean to frighten you.   Are you
okay?"   There stood Mr. Surly Jamison from the day before,
hard-hat and all.   But he didn't look surly now—he looked
concerned, and more than a little startled himself by Jolene's
splashy acknowledgment of his presence.

"What...How...What   are   *you*   doing   here?"   Jolene
managed to stammer.

"Well...and a gracious good morning to you, as well,"
Jamison replied with an aristocratic nod of his head, and a
playful twinkle in his eye.

Jolene felt like a fool.   "I'm...I'm sorry.   I didn't mean
to be rude."   Then her disposition kicked in. "But you *did*
creep up on me in my own backyard, unannounced.   How
did you know where I live, anyway?"

"I called the station."

Jolene eyed him even more suspiciously then.   "No
way.   There's no way anybody at the station would tell a
stranger where I lived."

"But I'm not a stranger," Jamison smiled, putting his
forefinger under the rim of his hard-hat, pushing it back on
his head.   "I'm the subject of your interview yesterday,
remember?   At least that's what your records at the station
show.   I told them there was some material for the interview
I had forgotten to give you, and they told me you were
working at home today and gave me the address."

Jolene silently thanked her unknown benefactor at the
station, vowing to find out who it was, and give him a piece
of her mind.

"All right, then." Jolene crossed her arms.   "Now that
you're here, what do you want?"   But crossing her arms was
a mistake.   When she let go of the chair, she started to
wobble again.

"Right now, I think I want to get you a seat," Jamison
replied, swiftly pulling out the chair so Jolene could hop to it,

and once again sit down at the table. Jamison casually sat down in the chair next to her, removing his hard hat, and placing it on the table.

"Mr. Jamison," Jolene began, mustering her composure, "at the risk of repeating myself—*what are you doing here?*"

"Hi!" came a greeting from near Jamison's elbow. Curious about their visitor, Zayna had come over to the table. Starting with her father, Zayna had twisted men around her baby finger with just a smile since birth. Something about the adorable child seemed to just naturally kindle their paternalistic instinct. She flashed Jamison a particularly brilliant smile now. It worked as infallibly as ever.

"Hello, honey!" Jamison replied, instantly taken. "Aren't you a cutie-pie! What's your name?"

Zayna, charmer supreme, promptly answered, "Zayna JoAnne Jeffries."

"What a pretty name," Jamison told her.

"Thank you. I'm named after my mommy and daddy. And my middle name is a meditation from my grandmothers' names," Zayna importantly informed him.

"That's 'combination,' honey," Jolene couldn't help but put in.

"Com-bin-a-tion," Zayna carefully agreed. Having exhausted that subject, she turned to more immediate matters. "Gee-Gee, can I have some juice?"

"*May* I have some juice," Jolene instructed. "Yes, you may." Jolene started to shakily rise, but it was a tough go. "Mr. Jamison..." she said stiffly, "if you'll excuse us, I'm going back in now. I'm sure you can find your way back to the front of..."

"Look, you just sit tight. I'll get the juice for your daughter," Jamison volunteered, rising.

"I'm not her daughter," Zayna said, giggling. "I'm her *granddaughter!*" She leaned toward Jamison, "That means she's my Daddy's mommy—not *my* mommy," she patiently explained.

Jamison looked at Jolene in surprise, "*You're* a grandmother?"

Jolene returned his stare head-on. "Yes, I am.   And proud of it."   She couldn't help but smile at his stupefaction. "A few of us still have our own teeth, you know."

Jamison was taken aback a moment, then threw back his head and laughed.   "So I see," he chuckled.   He leaned closer, looking into Jolene's eyes.   "And a very beautiful smile, too," he finished softly.

Jolene couldn't take her eyes from his.   But Zayna broke the silence by piping up, "Can...may I have my juice, now—please?"

Jamison tore his gaze from Jolene. "You sure can, sugar. I'll get it for you."   He eyed Jolene's coffee cup.   "And it looks like your grandmother could use a refill on her coffee, too."   He took the coffee cup and started for the patio doors.

Jolene protested.   "Hey, wait a minute!   You can't just..."

"Oh, yes, I can," Jamison replied.   He stopped and smiled disarmingly down at Jolene.   "But the question is if I *may*."   He gestured towards the door and the kitchen beyond.   "May I?"

Is this the same man I met yesterday? Jolene wondered. She ought to send him on his way she knew, but... "Uh...well...I hate to trouble you...I..."

"No trouble at all," Jamison replied, going into the kitchen with her coffee cup.

What am I doing letting a strange man ramble around in my kitchen? Jolene thought uneasily.   *Here I sit in my bathrobe, barely able to walk, and with a small child to protect to boot.   I barely know this man at all.*

But that wasn't exactly true.   Jolene knew quite a bit

about Jamison—his professional life at least—from her preparations for the interview. He and a group of his friends in the construction business had grown tired of working for other people and started a business of their own.

But their construction company, H.O.M.E., was not your usual construction company. Thus far, they dealt exclusively in home renovation. With all the boarded-up, neglected houses around town, Jamison had gotten the idea of buying the properties, fixing them up, and reselling them. The company made a reasonable profit for themselves, yet maintained prices affordable for most mid to lower income families.

From when she first heard about it, Jolene had wanted to cover this story. She admired the ingenuity and guts of the men tackling the project. It wasn't easy to give up good-paying jobs to strike out on your own. And she also admired the manner in which they gave back to the community, turning eye-sore fire traps into respectable homes for people who otherwise would not have been able to afford a house at all.

"Gee-Gee? Gee-Gee!" Jolene was brought out of her rumination by Zayna tugging on the sleeve of her robe. "Gee-Gee, who is *that?*" Zayna wanted to know, pointing into the kitchen, from which issued the sounds of dishes precariously rattling.

"That's Mr. Jamison, Zee."

"So he's not..." Zayna lowered her voice to a whisper, "a *stranger?*" Zayna queried.

Jolene could almost hear Zayna's active little mind working. The child was friendly—too friendly. Lately, Jolene had been especially emphatic in cautioning Zayna about strangers. It wouldn't do to admit grandmother had allowed one into their very midst.

"No, honey. He's not a stranger. I met him yesterday

for my TV show."

Satisfied, Zayna ran toward the swings again, just as Jamison exited the kitchen with a tray.

"Hey, wait!   Don't you want your juice?" Jamison asked, placing the tray on the table with one hand as he held out a cup in the other.

Jolene was astonished.   He had actually gotten one of Zayna's special cups, the plastic ones with spouted tops. Since they were outdoors, Jolene wasn't concerned about Zayna spilling her drink.   It was just that Zayna wouldn't use any other kind of cup.   These were "her" cups.   Jolene realized she should have mentioned this to Jamison.   She was surprised at him having the acumen to find one of the little yellow cups with the duckies on the side.

It looked somehow incongruous, this powerful, strapping man, gracefully crouching and sitting back on his heels to give Zayna her drink.   The small brightly colored cup was almost lost in his large, calloused hand.

Then he smiled at the child.   Zayna giggled as she smiled back, reaching for the cup.   And Jolene was transfixed, her mind taking a snapshot of the big man handing the cup to the tiny child on her own level, and with such gentleness.   The golden glow of the early morning sun cast a luminescence over the two, and Jolene's heart was forever branded by the imprint of this fleeting, touching tableau.

The moment was broken as Zayna laughed, and happily skipped off to the swing once again.

Standing, Jamison turned to the tray.   It bore not one, but two cups of coffee, a carafe, and sugar and cream, as well as spoons and napkins.

"I hope you don't mind," Jamison said, gesturing to his own cup, and taking his seat once again.   "I thought maybe we could talk over a cup of coffee..." He smiled at Jolene as he handed over her cup, "since you've declared me 'not a stranger.' "

"That was for my granddaughter's sake," Jolene replied, peering closely into Jamison's eyes.   "Personally, I think you're one of the strangest men I ever met."

Far than being offended, Jamison actually seemed rather pleased by this assessment.   "Oh, really?"   He grinned as he leaned back in his chair, and lifted one work booted ankle over the opposite blue-jeaned knee, "How so?"

"You nearly bite my head off yesterday, and then you pop up here today trying to charm me to death."

Jamison leaned forward, eyes twinkling, but with a spark of true inquiry in his voice, "Well...how am I doing?"

Jolene caught her breath at the candid captivation in his gaze.   *He's...he's* flirting *with me!*   Jolene dropped her eyes quickly.   *No, he's not,* another internal voice scolded.   *The man's just trying to be nice.   My goodness, has it been that long since you've been with an attractive man that now you're seeing things that aren't there?*   Jolene didn't know which voice to believe.   She didn't look up.   She didn't want Jamison to see the confusion she knew her eyes would reveal.

Jamison uncrossed his legs and reached between his knees with one hand to quickly grab the seat of his chair and scoot it forward, closer to Jolene's.   "Look, Mrs. Jeffries...Jolene...I acted like an ass yesterday.   I was trying to do about five different things at once on only about four hours sleep the night before.   That's the reason I acted that way.   The reason.   Not the excuse.   There *is* no excuse for acting that way—especially to a lady, a sister."   He leaned even closer.   "I'm sorry."

Jolene looked up then.   And there could be no mistaking the sincerity of his apology.   He was watching her closely, cautiously, as though hoping for the best, but expecting the worse.

And her heart melted.   His gentle friendliness of the past half hour had succeeded in overcoming the shadow of yesterday.   "Well," Jolene said slowly, "anybody can have a bad day."   She smiled, "It's been rumored I have one myself every once in a while."

Jamison's gaze never wavered.   "I'm really sorry, Jolene.   Please...forgive me."

"Forgiven;   forgotten...Akron,"   Jolene   whispered, offering her hand, suddenly shy.

As they shook hands, Jolene could feel the strength in his fingers, and the roughness of his palm.   Her hand in his looked almost as small and defenseless as did Zayna's. Jolene looked up again, into his eyes.   She saw his relief, his thankfulness that she was willing to put the past behind them. And she saw...she saw...

"That's Ron...or Ohio," he said softly, his hand unwillingly releasing hers.

"Excuse me?"

"Nobody calls me Akron except my father.   Mostly it's Ron.   My buddies call me Ohio...for obvious reasons."

"Were you born there?   Akron, Ohio, I mean," Jolene asked.

"No.   Never been to Ohio in my life," Ron chuckled.

"Then why..."

"My dad heard the name Akron when my mother was carrying me.   It means 'ninth son.' "

"It does?   And are you?"

"Nope."   Ron picked up the coffee carafe and topped off first Jolene's cup, then his own.   "Actually, I was their *first* child.   Dad used to say he was counting in reverse order."   Ron laughed. "And he almost made it, too.   There wound up being eight of us."   He looked at Jolene playfully, "Although, of course, four were girls."

Jolene had to laugh along with him.   "So you were

raised with four younger sisters.   Is that why you're so good with little girls?" she nodded her head toward Zayna.

"I have a little girl of my own.   Although I know she'd go, 'Oh, *Daddy!*' if she heard me call her that.   She's fifteen now, going on twenty-five."   Jolene didn't understand the shadow that crossed Ron's face.

Ron saw the perplexity in Jolene's eyes.   "I lost my wife two years ago," he said softly.   It's...it's been...tough." Jolene could tell that was a profound understatement.   "And for a little girl..." he was continuing, "losing her mother..." he clearly didn't know just how to continue.

Jolene reached forward and covered his hand with hers. "I'm sorry," she said softly, not knowing what else to say.

Ron looked up and gave her a fragile smile as his other hand covered hers.   "And what about you?" he asked softly. He gently lifted Jolene's left hand.   "No wedding ring? Where's the little one's grandpa?"

"I...I don't know," Jolene stammered.   "We were divorced when my son was a baby.   My ex-husband just...just sort of disappeared."

"And your son?   Where is he?"   Ron, discerning that the subject of Jolene's marriage was off limits, deftly changed the subject.

"He and his wife are in Germany.   Zane's a career Air Force man," Jolene said.   Her pride in her son was unmistakable.   "In fact, he met Marlena in the service. She's career, too.   Zayna was born in Germany.   But as she got closer to school age, they were concerned about her not having exposure to her own culture, her own people." Jolene smiled over to where Zayna had left the swing in favor of the glider.   "So she's been with me for the past six months.   She's going to stay with me until her parents can get state-side orders."

Neither spoke for a moment, then Ron suddenly

declared, "Hey, have you had breakfast?"

"No," Jolene told him, not comprehending the sudden change in subject.

"Comin' right up."   Jamison stood, and headed once again for the kitchen.   "After all, since I was indirectly the cause of your...ah, somewhat limited mobility, the least I can do to fix breakfast for you."

"But Ron, that's not necessary," Jolene again attempted to rise.   "You don't have to..."

"Gee-Gee, I'm hungry."   Having heard the word "breakfast", Zayna had come over and felt obliged to put her bid in.

"I am, too," Ron told the child.   "Do you like omelets?"

"What's a om-lett?" Zayna wanted to know.

"Eggs," Ron responded.

"Oh.   Yes, I like eggs.   Especially bald eggs."

"That's *boiled* eggs, dear," Jolene corrected her.

"Eggs it is.   In an omelet for us..." Ron told Jolene, "and a couple of hairless ones for you," he touched a finger to the tip of Zayna's nose.

"But Ron..."

"Look, I'm hungry.   The baby is hungry.   Aren't you hungry?"

"Well, yes, I am, but you can't..."

"Considering your delicate condition," he pointed to Jolene's ankle, "and the fact that Zayna can't reach the counter top looks like I'm the only one here who can."   He smiled and offered Jolene his arm.   "That is...if I may."

I shouldn't Jolene told herself.   *I don't know this man. But I was just barely able to fix myself coffee and hop out here.   And it's not like I know nothing about the man.   And he's been so gracious it would actually be rude to refuse. And...* But then her alter-ego spoke up, *Be honest with yourself, girl.   You* want *to. And, hell, what's wrong with that?*   Before she could stop herself, Jolene laughed, and took Ron's arm, leaning on his strong shoulder as he helped her into the kitchen.

Excusing herself, Jolene carefully made her way to the bedrooms, to quickly dress and supervise Zayna, who insisted on dressing herself.   That having been accomplished, Zayna ran into the living room to check out Sesame Street while Jolene settled at the kitchen table.

"More coffee?" Ron asked, standing at the sink, washing his hands.

"No, thanks," Jolene replied.   "Two cups is my limit. More than that, and I start to vibrate."

Ron laughed.   "I should probably lay off the stuff more myself.   I drink it all day long.   It's hard for me to fall asleep at night sometimes."

He had placed eggs, milk, and butter, as well as a tin of Hungry Jack biscuits on the counter.   "Ah!   My favorites!" he declared, adroitly tossing the biscuit tin in the air, catching it behind his back.   "I see you are a woman of rare taste and refinement."   He smiled warmly at Jolene, "But I guess I already knew that."

Jolene watched in fascination as he expertly moved about the kitchen, starting the biscuits and mixing the omelet with not an iota of wasted motion.   "Sausage or bacon?" he asked, peering into the refrigerator.

"Bacon.   It's Zayna's favorite."

"Mine, too."

In no time he had the bacon sizzling and was chopping onion and green pepper for the omelet.   "Light on the peppers," Jolene cautioned.   "Our friend's not real fond of them."

"Oh.   Glad you reminded me.   I believe the princess wanted to go the Humpty Dumpty route, anyway."   He got out a small saucepan and set two eggs to boiling.

"Ron, you're amazing," Jolene marveled.   "You really know your way around a kitchen.   You must do a lot of cooking."

"Yeah."   His happy-go-lucky manner seemed to deflate.   "I've been doing most of the cooking at my place...for a while now."

Jolene could have kicked herself.   "That was thoughtless of me, Ron.   I'm sorry."

His face was openly vulnerable as he studied Jolene a moment before answering, "It's okay, Jolene.   It's just that it jumps up and catches me by ambush sometimes.   You'd think that after two years..."

"I don't think time is a factor," Jolene said softly, looking out the patio door.   "I don't think you ever just get used to losing someone you love."

The obvious intensity of Jolene's words made Ron pause, and look at her in contemplation.   Just as he was about to speak, the timer went off, and he hurried to remove the biscuits from the oven.

Ron wouldn't even allow Jolene to set the table, following her direction to locate the plates and silverware.

"Breakfast is ready, little one," he called to Zayna, who didn't have to be told twice.   After serving the ladies, Ron took a seat.

"Everything looks wonderful, Ron," Jolene told him, sincerely meaning it.

"Not bad, even if I do say so myself," Ron agreed, rubbing his hands together.   "Could you pass the jam?"

"No.   Not yet," Zayna advised him in a whisper. "First we have to say prayers."

"Oh.   Right.   Sorry."   Ron accordingly bowed his head, after casting an abashed glance Jolene's way.

Zayna bowed hers as well, and solemnly said, "God is great.   God is good.   Let us bank Him.   Pour the food.

Amen."

"That's 'thank Him', honey," Jolene gently reminded, leaving a critique of the rest for another day.

The meal was marvelous, the company making the food taste particularly appetizing.   Just as they were finishing, Jolene changing her mind and consenting to share another cup of coffee with Ron, the doorbell rang.

"Who could that be so early in the morning?" Jolene wondered aloud.   She excused herself and went to the door. There stood a very tall, very handsome, very dusty young man who looked somehow familiar.   "Yes?" Jolene asked. " May I help you?"

The young man hastily snatched off the baseball cap that was perched backwards on his head.   "Yes, ma'am.   I hope so.   Good morning.   I'm glad I found the right house.   Ah, you're Mrs. Jeffries, from Channel Seven, right?"

"Yes, I am.   Do I know you?   Have we met before?"

"No, ma'am, we haven't.   Although I've watched you on the tube so often it sort of feels like it—to me at least.   I'm LaSalles Jamison.   I'm looking for my Dad.   The guys at the site told me he might be here."

No wonder he looks so familiar, Jolene reflected.   *He's a younger, even taller version of Ron.   But what would he be doing here?*   "Oh, so you work with your father?" Jolene said aloud.

"Yes, during the summer, and school holiday breaks.   I go to Ingram State."   He paused and stood a bit taller.   "I'll be a senior this fall."

"Good for you," Jolene told him with a smile.   "Your father's in the kitchen.   Please, come in."

LaSalles stepped tenuously over the threshold.   "I'd better not come in too far.   Been working around cement this morning.   I'm sorta grubby."   LaSalles was an inch or so taller than Ron, but not as muscular as his father.   Still, he was a robust specimen of young manhood.

"Don't worry about it.   You're fine," Jolene said kindly. "Won't you have a seat?"

"No, I'd better not.   I'll just wait here," LaSalles told her, staying close to the door.

"Okay.   Just a moment.   I'll tell your father you're here."   Jolene went as quickly as she could back into the kitchen.   "Ron, your son's at the door."

Ron was surprised.   "He is?   But what..."   He glanced quickly at his watch.   "Hot damn!   I didn't realize the time."   Ron jumped up and grabbed his hard-hat.   "I gotta get back to the site."

Ron followed Jolene into the living room, where Zayna had already moved in on LaSalles, having asked him to hold her Cabbage Patch doll while she got her toy stroller out of the front closet.

"Getting in a little practice, son?" Ron said with a wry smile as he approached the door.

LaSalles squirmed uncomfortably, clearly embarrassed. "Aw, Dad, come on.   Give me a break."

Zayna stepped forward then and took the doll back. "Thank you for holding my baby," she said, looking gratefully up at LaSalles.

Despite his chagrin, LaSalles gave her a big smile in return, "You're welcome, sweetheart."   He turned his attention to Ron.   "Dad, Ernie told me you'd come by to talk to Mrs. Jefferies.   He remembered you said she lived on Village Drive.   I saw your truck in the driveway.   But we thought you'd be right back.   The building inspector's coming out this morning to okay the foundation on the Maple street house."

"That's right!" Ron exclaimed, smacking his forehead with the heel of his palm.   "I'm sorry, Les.   I forgot.   Has he come by yet?"

"No, but he'll be there any minute.   You *forgot?*" LaSalles looked at Ron closely.   "That's not like you, Dad. What up?"

"Nothing, son, nothing," Ron said hastily.   He turned, "I hate to eat and run.   Thank you for breakfast, Jolene." At this, one of LaSalles eyebrows shot up.

"No, thank you, Ron," Jolene asserted.   "After all, you did all the cooking."   LaSalles turned to look at his father in bewilderment.

"Anytime.   It was my pleasure," Ron told her, the expression in his eyes validating the fact that this was no idle compliment.

"I think I'll be out and about again in a day or two.   Can we reschedule your interview for later this week?" Jolene asked.

"You bet.   I'll be looking forward to it."

So will I, Jolene thought.

"Well," Ron said, lingering at the door, "talk to you soon."

"Okay."   Jolene turned, "Nice to have met you, LaSalles."

"Same here," LaSalles replied, looking back and forth between Jolene and his father.   "Come on, Dad.   We better get on the good foot if we're going to beat that inspector to the site."

"Right."   Ron settled his hardhat on his head.   "See you, Jolene," he said softly.

"'Bye."   Jolene shut the door after them, but just before it closed heard LaSalles say, "Uh, Dad...*breakfast?*"

CHAPTER 2

"So you've been in business a year and a half now?"

"Yes—officially.   But we've been doing various projects on a freelance basis for about seven years, while each of us was still working our regular jobs."

"That had to be tough."

"Yes, it was.   I'm a carpenter, Ernie a plumber, Hakeem an electrician, and Mike a bricklayer.   We got to know each other through working various jobs together.   Then we started calling each other in on the different private jobs we did evenings.

"But it's been even tougher since we went into business for ourselves."   Ron flashed Jolene that killer smile.   "You never work as hard for anybody else as you do for yourself."

Jolene looked back at the newly poured concrete foundation, and the skeleton of a frame rising from it, "And this project is your first *new* home?"

"Right.   Up to now we've just been remodeling and restoring pre-existing homes."   Ron nodded toward the structure, "This is the first one we've built from scratch." He paused, looking at the framework with pride.   "It's my own design."

"It is?"   Jolene was surprised.   "So you're an architect?"

"Not yet.   I've been taking classes at night for years, but I had to stop when we decided to start H.O.M.E.   But now that the business is going so well, I plan to start back in the fall.   I only need a few more credits before I can get my degree and certification."

"That's wonderful.   You are certainly an outstanding role model," Jolene was truly impressed, and as she looked up into Ron's eyes she momentarily forgot they were on camera.   A beat passed before she remembered where she was, and hastily asked, "And you named the company H.O.M.E. because you work exclusively on home, rather than commercial, construction?"

"Yes, that, and also it's an acronym for the four of us guys: Hakeem, Ohio—that's what the guys call me..." Jolene already knew this, but Ron knew their audience didn't, "Mike, and Ernie," Ron went on.

"Your story is absolutely fascinating, Mr. Jamison. Thank you for sharing it.   And we wish you and your partners only the best in the future."

"Thank you."

Jolene turned to face Frank and the camera, "This is Jolene Jeffries with Channel Seven's weekly feature, 'Window on Our World,' spotlighting our community's citizens on the move."   She waited until the red light on the camera went off.   "Okay, Frank, that's a wrap."

"Right, JJ," Frank replied, taking Jolene's microphone, and winding up the cord.   He turned to Ron.   "I need a few minutes to get some lead-in shots.   Is that all right, Mr. Jamison?"

"Sure.   No problem.   Need me to go with you?" Ron asked.

"No, thanks, I'm fine.   I'll be right back, Double J." Frank ambled off with the camera, seeking just the right scenes for the program's opening and closing shots.

"Well, Ron," Jolene said, "the interview went wonderfully..."   She smiled wryly, looking down at her now recuperated ankle, "since we got off on the right foot this time."

Ron laughed.   "Yes...and I see you've got more suitable gear on that 'right foot,' this time," he teased, checking out Jolene's sturdy brogans.

Jolene gave him a roguish smile.   "I don't make the same mistakes twice, Mr. Jamison.   But seriously, Ron, the interview was great.   Thank you."

"No, thank *you*," Ron insisted.   "We don't have much of a publicity budget.   We've mostly been getting by on word of mouth.   The exposure is appreciated."

"You deserve it.   This is a tremendous human interest story.   You're doing a true service to the community, fixing up those old houses.   Not to mention all the families you've helped.   Your company could get more for the houses you've renovated than you've been asking, you know."

"Yeah, I know.   But our intention is just to make a respectable profit, not to make a killing, especially at the expense of those who can least afford it."   Ron gave her that smile again.   "We're needy, but not greedy.   And it's kind of a mutual thing.   We're tapping a market that's mostly of people who otherwise wouldn't be buying homes at all.   So we get their business, and they get a decent place to live."

"I...I think it's wonderful of you, " Jolene looked up, and again got momentarily lost in the depths of Ron's smoldering black eyes.   "Uh...of all of you guys," she finished unsteady, suddenly looking away.   "Well, I'd...better be going.   I'll call and let you know when the show is going to air."

"Aren't you forgetting something?" Ron asked with a smile, staring at the hard-hard Jolene was still wearing.

"Oh.   Yes, of course!" Jolene reached up, but Ron beat her to it.

"Allow me," he said softly, gently lifting the protective covering from her head.   His hands lingered for a moment. "You know, since we first met, I've just been yearning to touch your hair."   He moved a step closer, "It *is* just as soft as it looks."

"T..thank you," Jolene whispered in reply.   She felt agitated under the deep scrutiny of his gaze.   But it was a pleasant sort of agitation.   She found it difficult to look away.

"Come on."   Ron took her elbow.   "I'll see you to the van."

They walked along in silence for a short while, until Ron said, "Uh...Double J?"

Jolene laughed, "That's what they call me at the station since I always initial all my memos 'JJ'.   In fact, that's why Zayna calls me 'Gee-Gee'," she went on.   "Her parents got leave when she was about a year old and came to visit.   She heard some of my friends from the station calling me JJ and tried to say it, too.   But it came out 'Gee-Gee'."   Jolene laughed again, "My rascal of a son made it stick by saying it stood for 'gorgeous grandma'."

"How right he was," Ron put in, smiling down at Jolene.

By this time they had reached the station's van.   Ron's smile suddenly faded.   He seemed suddenly jittery, unsure of himself.   "Jolene...I was wondering...that is..." he stammered.   Ron took a deep breath, "Look, Jolene, what I'm trying to say is I'd...I'd really like to see you again."

Jolene was caught off guard. Another woman might have picked up on Ron's signals, but Jolene had convinced herself it was merely her imagination, her own wishful thinking.   Now here it was.   It was really happening.   She was so unprepared, she blurted out the first thing to cross her mind: "Why?"

"Huh?" Now it was Ron who was caught unaware. "Uh...why not?   I mean, why *shouldn't* I want to see you again?"

"Ron, I wasn't aware that you felt...I mean..."

"Jolene," Ron moved a little closer.   "I haven't seen a lady since...in a long time.   I guess I'm kinda of out practice. But I've been hitting on you the best I know how since we first met."   He took her hand and looked deeply into her eyes.   "Do you mean to tell me my rap is so rusty that you didn't even know?" he finished softly, only partially in jest.

Jolene looked down at their joined hands. She didn't know what to say, how to answer him. She couldn't say what she *had* thought—that she was powerfully attracted to him, but thought it was strictly one way.

When she didn't speak, Ron slowly released her hand. "Jolene, I'm sorry." He was clearly embarrassed. "What would a woman like you want with a guy like me, struggling to hold a new business together—and his family, to boot. I shouldn't have been so presumptuous. But I thought...At least, I'd hoped..."

Jolene looked up quickly then. "Ron, any woman would be flattered by the attention of a man like you...." she said softly. She didn't know what to say next. Jolene was seldom in this predicament. She made her living communicating. But that was different. That was TV. This was real life.

"...but..." Ron prompted, looking at her with wounded eyes, preparing himself for disappointment.

Jolene was touched by his evident dejection at what he thought was a rebuff. "But you're not the only one out of practice," she said with a gentle smile. "Seems I've forgotten how to accept a gentleman's invitation. At least, so that he *knows* I'm accepting his invitation."

A slow grin materialized on Ron's face, "Yeah?"

Jolene grinned shyly back, "Yeah."

They stood contemplating each other for an instant, both enthralled by the magic of the moment. Then Ron said softly, "In that case, I was wondering if..."

"Okay," Frank was back. "Got the stuff I needed. Ready to go, JJ?"

"Ah...yes, Frank," Jolene said, quickly switching gears.

"All right, then. Let's roll." Frank said, placing the camera and other equipment in the back of the van. He walked to the driver's door and got behind the wheel. "Nice to meet you, Mr. Jamison," Frank called as he started the engine.

"Same here," Ron called to him. He turned to Jolene, "Look, we're having a barbecue at my place tomorrow evening. No big deal, just a few family, and friends. Would you and Zayna like to come?"

Out of the corner of her eye, Jolene could see Frank watching them, obviously fascinated by this turn of events, and as deeply into the conversation and she and Ron. But then she looked into Ron's eyes, and suddenly she didn't care *who* was watching. "Yes, Ron. Sounds like fun. We'd love to come."

"Great!" Ron was beaming now. He opened the door of the van for Jolene. "I'll pick you up about six o'clock, okay?"

Jolene smiled back, "Fine."

Ron helped Jolene up the step into the van and closed the door. "See you tomorrow." He stood waving as the van drove away.

There was silence in the van for several moments, Frank stealing glances at Jolene with a silly grin on his face. Finally, Jolene turned to him, "*What*?"

"What? Don't 'what' me, Double J. You know 'what.' You and this guy practically come to blows the other day, and now he's asking you for a date? And you *accepting?* What's wrong with this picture?"

"What's wrong is someone sticking his nose into places it doesn't belong," Jolene sniffed, nonchalantly looking out the side window.

"Aw, come on, Jo, this is me, Frank, your devoted friend and co-worker for the past six years." Frank nudged Jolene with his elbow. "Spill it."

"Spill what? Ron invited Zee and me over for a family barbecue. That hardly qualifies as being whisked away to the Kasbah."

"It does for a woman who hasn't had a date since Hector was a pup. Don't get me wrong, Jo.   Jamison seems like a straight up dude.   And it's about time you got yourself a man."

"Like that buddy of yours that you sicced on me last year?" Jolene came back with a wry smile.

"Oh, JJ, gimme a break.   The guy was on my bowling team.   He seemed okay.   When he found out I worked with you he asked for an introduction.   How was I to know he was a pervert?"

"Pervert is right.   He seemed okay to me, too—at first. But when he brought me home, the wrestling match we had in his car could have made it to pay-per-view.   I had to knee him where the sun don't shine just to make him back off."

"Yeah, I know," Frank chuckled.   "He was walking bent over for a week.   No better for him.   I would have punched him out if you hadn't already settled his hash.   But stop changing the subject.   How did you and 'Ron' get so chummy so fast?"

"Can I help it if the man has exceptional taste in women?" Jolene flippantly replied.   But she didn't feel very flippant.   Now that she'd had a moment to reflect she wondered if she was doing the right thing.   She was drawn to Ron, and now she knew he felt the same about her.

But we're not kids.   We're two mature people with families and careers and responsibilities, her thoughts rambled on.   *With so much else going on in our lives, how can we make a place in them for each other?*

"Ron, I could have driven us over," Jolene said as they cruised down the street in Ron's quad-cab pick-up.   "Then you wouldn't have had to leave your company to come for us."

Ron just chuckled, "I don't have 'company,' Jolene. Everybody there is someone I've known for years—or all my life. And I doubt they've even missed me." He grinned over at her, "I'm forty-eight years old. I'm in the generation of men who are used to calling for ladies they've invited out for the evening. I'm too old to change now."

"Well, you're only a year older than I am, so don't put yourself in the rocking chair set just yet." Jolene laughed nervously, looking pensively out the side window.

They rode on in silence for a while before Ron asked, "What's the matter, Jo?"

"Nothing. Nothing, Ron."

"Jolene, I haven't known you very long, but I know *something's* bothering you. Is it the truck? I guess I should have borrowed my son's car, but..."

"No. No, Ron. Why would I mind the truck?" Jolene smiled over at Ron. "This is fun."

"It sure is!" Zayna enthusiastically agreed, bouncing up and down on the pick-up's tiny rear seat. "I like riding up high! I can *see* everything!"

"Just make sure with all that bouncing you 'see' your way into staying in your booster seat and keeping that seat belt fastened, young lady," Jolene cautioned.

"Is that why you've been so quiet back there, princess?" Ron asked.

"Uh-huh. I like this. I can't see *nothing* in grandma's car," Zayna replied, going back to her rapt review of the passing scenery.

"Well, at least I've pleased *one* of my dates this evening." He looked uncertainly over to Jolene. "I'm not so sure about the other one."

"Ron...it's just that...well, I'm a bit nervous about

meeting your...your family."

"Why?   I've met *your* family."   He smiled and gestured with his head toward the back seat, where Zayna still had her nose pressed to the window.

Jolene had to laugh.   "That's hardly the same.   You've completely mesmerized Zayna, and you know it."

"And you'll completely mesmerize my family."   He took Jolene's hand.   "Just like you've already mesmerized me," he finished softly.

Jolene smiled back, "Well, at least I've already met one member of your family— your son."

"That's right.   And this shindig is basically for him— and his fiancée."

"Fiancée?   But he seems so young.   And he told me he was getting his degree next year."

"He is.   He and Shandra are both students at Ingram State.   That's where they met.   She'll be a senior next year also.   But she may not graduate on time."

Before Jolene could inquire further, Ron was pulling the truck to the curb.   "Okay, ladies, we have arrived," he told them, hopping down from the running board to the street. Ron went to the passenger side and helped Jolene alight before lifting Zayna from the rear.

Zayna clung to Ron, "Will you give me a piggy-back ride?   My Daddy always used to before he went away," she finished wistfully.

"Princess, it would be an honor."   Ron swung Zayna around to his back, where she promptly wrapped her arms around his neck.   "This way, Jolene," he said, gesturing down the sidewalk to the left.

"Oh," Jolene said, following his lead.   "I thought *this* was your house."   She pointed to the neat, but rather ordinary ranch house where he had parked in front.

"No.   I'm further on down the street."   Jolene noted

with quiet approval that Ron had taken care to cross behind her, so he was walking on the curbside of the sidewalk. The man truly did have old-fashioned manners—and the good sense to use them.

"I was parked in the driveway when I left, but I knew somebody would grab my spot before I got back," Ron shook his head in good-natured resignation.

True enough, there were cars, trucks, and vans lining both sides of the street as well as packed into the circular driveway of a large rambling house a few doors down. Ron turned into this driveway a few moments later.

"Ron! What a beautiful house!" Jolene exclaimed.

And it was. An old Victorian manor, it was perfectly restored and carefully maintained. Jolene loved the wide L-shaped veranda that spanned the front and right side of the house. Graceful cornices and intricate lattice-work in a cheery green adorned the porch roof ledge and the three gables, each jauntily sporting a dormer window. The green trim made the spotlessly white house seem to sparkle that much more.

"Look, Gee-Gee," Zayna cried, pointing over Ron's shoulder with glee. "It's a castle!"

"No, baby," Ron chuckled as he settled Zayna on the ground. "It's not a castle. It's where I live."

"Well, that's what they say a man's home *is*—his castle," Jolene said, still admiring the lovely structure before them.

Zayna looked up at Ron with huge, awe-struck eyes, "Are you a king?" she whispered.

Ron laughed gently. "No, honey, I'm not." He looked over to Jolene. "But right now I sure feel like one."

The unmistakable smell of barbecue was in the air, along with the sounds of chatter and laughter. The Temptations' "My Girl" was playing in the background. Ron led them to the side of the house and along the porch.

The back yard was a flurry of activity.   People were talking in groups, walking around or sitting at tables or in lawn chairs on the grass.   A husky young man was at a table to the side, on which was a CD player and two of the biggest speakers Jolene had ever seen.

A group of people were dancing on the large concrete patio.   Jolene had to smile.   The ages of the dancers had to span 50 years. There was a white-haired gentleman smoothly guiding a teenage girl in an elegant ballroom move.   Next to them were a couple of kids in baggy jeans busting some moves that looked almost physically impossible.

There was a large gas grill bearing a tantalizing array of ribs and chicken.   LaSalles was at the grill, wearing a white bib apron bearing the logo, *ALL THE KIND WORDS, ALL THE GOOD WISHES, JUST CAN'T REPLACE HELP WITH THE DISHES.*   Seeing Jolene, he waved a long fork, "Hey, Mrs. Jefferies!   Hi!"

At that, everyone turned.   Despite all her experience in the public eye, Jolene felt tremendously self-conscious.

"Now, now, none of that," Ron said, seeming to sense her discomfort.   He put his arm lightly around her waist to lead her forward.   "They don't bite—at least, not until they know you better."

Zayna needed no such prompting.   She immediately went up to a group of children playing in a sandbox shaped like a big green turtle, sat down, and started chattering away.

Ron guided Jolene over to the grill.   "Uh, Les...where's Ernie?" Ron asked, looking down at the grill anxiously.

"Had to make a pit stop, Dad.   He'll be back in a minute.   Mrs. Jefferies, glad you could come," LaSalles said, blinking as smoke was getting in his eyes.

"Thanks for having us.   And please, call me Jolene." She deeply inhaled.   "That food looks absolutely mouth-watering."

"It won't stay that way for long if we leave Sir Burns-A-Lot in charge," a voice said from behind them. A rather short, stocky man stepped up to the grill. "Okay, I'm back now. Better let me take back over before this stuff gets carbonated."

"No problem there," LaSalles instantly agreed and started untying the apron.

Jolene recognized the man as the one who called to Ron on her first visit to the site. He offered his hand to Jolene, "Mrs. Jefferies, I'm Ernie Hill, one of Ohio's partners. Sorry I didn't get to meet you before."

"It's Jolene, Ernie. Nice to meet you. And it was a pleasure doing the story on H.O.M.E. It's such a great idea I'm surprised nobody's thought of it before."

"Oh, it's been done before, Jolene," Ernie told her. "Just not the way *we're* doing it. You know that a lot of the old office buildings downtown are being renovated into lofts?"

"Yes. We did a feature on it."

"Did you check out the price tags for those babies?" Ernie shook his head. "Most working folks can't afford fancy digs like that. There's a huge national construction company behind that project. And they're charging all the traffic will bear. And when they get a contract or a grant from the city to clean up old houses, they clean them up all right. They usually raze them to the ground, or build a parking lot or a party store..." He looked at Jolene closely, "especially in *our* neighborhoods."

Jolene blinked. "You're right. I...I just never looked at it that way before."

"We can't stop it from happening, but we can damn sure put a dent in it. Especially after we get that grant from the city."

"Grant? What grant?" Jolene asked.

"I didn't mention it because we just decided to go for it after our interview, Jolene," Ron told her.   "Those conglomerates have had a virtual monopoly on the city's renovation grants—until now.   We're gotten large enough now to put in a competitive bid for a grant."

"Ron, that's wonderful!" Jolene exclaimed.   "There're so many wonderful houses, houses like yours, that you could save with that kind of backing."

"That's what we think, too, Jo.   And it would also allow us to create some jobs and hire more people.   So we're going to give it our best shot."

By this time LaSalles had finally wiggled his way out of the apron and handed it to Ernie, who then began to put it on himself.

"Hey, man.   You don't have to do that," Ron protested. "You're our guest.   I just wanted you to take over for me while I was gone.   I've got it."

"No, you don't," Ernie insisted, putting the apron over his head.   "I *know* you're not trying to treat me like 'company' or something.   Hell, I got the toilets working in this old dinosaur after you bought it!"   Ernie looked over at Jolene.   "Besides, if I had a lady this fine on *my* arm, I bet I'd find a better way to keep her entertained!"

Ron laughed and clapped him on the shoulder.   "My man, you do have a point.   Thanks."   He turned to Jolene, "Let me introduce you around, Jo."

They mingled with the group.   Jolene met Ron's other partners and their families.   Ron's sister, Habiba, seemed particularly happy to meet Jolene.   "It's so wonderful you came!   I'm looking forward to watching the story you did on Ron and the guys.   And you're a grandmother!" Habiba babbled on.   "I can't believe it.   Your little granddaughter is just adorable!   She's over at the children's table with my kids."

"Thank you," Jolene managed to squeeze in.   "She..."

"Well, I guess we have a lot of young attractive grandmothers these days," Habiba laughed.   "You're even prettier in person than you are on TV—*isn't* she, Ron?" she added pointedly.

"Now, Bebe, don't get started," Ron sighed.   "You..."

"All he does is work," Habiba went on to Jolene, as though Ron hadn't spoken.   "I've been telling him for the longest, get out and enjoy yourself sometime.   Find yourself a nice woman, and..."

"Come on, Lene.   Let me introduce you to my Dad. Excuse us, Bebe."   Ron took Jolene's hand and steered her away, leaving Habiba in mid-sentence.

"Sorry about that," Ron whispered as they approached a cluster of tables.   "Bebe has a heart of gold, but she's designated herself the family match-maker, and..."

"And she's looking out for her big brother," Jolene finished for him.   "That's what sisters do."

Ron smiled down at Jolene, "Are you always this perceptive and understanding?"   He was teasing, but there was some seriousness behind his words.

"Yes," Jolene teased back.   "Especially at family barbecues."

By this time they'd reached the tables.   The older man Jolene had seen dancing so smoothly stood as they approached.   "Jolene, this is my father, Walter Jamison. Dad, this is..."

"Son, I know who this lovely lady is.   Pleased to meet you, Mrs. Jeffries."

"Please call me Jolene, Mr. Jamison.   The pleasure is mine."

"Then you have to call me Walt.   Won't you have a seat?"   As Walt held out a chair for Jolene, she couldn't help but reflect, *Now I know why Ron has such gentlemanly manners.*

"I was watching you on the dance floor, Mr...ah, Walt. You're a marvelous dancer."

"Thank you, my dear, but that must have been my brother, William.   I just got here."   At Jolene's puzzled look, he added, "We're twins."

"Oh," Jolene said.   "I'm sorry."

"That's okay, honey.   People been mistaking one of us for the other for seventy-two years now.   I'm used to it." Walt gave Jolene a wink.   "Anyway, I'm a better dancer than he is.   Before she passed away, Akron's mother and I used to cut a fine figure on the dance-floor."   He looked at Jolene closely.   "Do you dance?"

"Not nearly as well as you...ah, your brother, but I took ballroom lessons at the Y last year.   It was fun."

The DJ had put on Freddie Jackson's "Jam Tonight". "This is a good ballroom song," Walt said rising.   He extended his hand to Jolene, "May I have the pleasure?"

Jolene was startled.   "Walt, I...haven't danced in a long time.   I don't know if I..."

"Better tell him yes, Lene," Ron advised.   He doesn't take no for answer..."   Ron leaned in closer, eyes twinkling. "Like his son."

Jolene laughed and took Walt's hand.   He led her to the dance floor.   Before Jolene had a chance to get nervous, Walt put an arm around her and guided her skillfully into the dance.   Although she didn't consider herself that good at it, Jolene had always loved to dance.   She realized now just how much she had missed it.

Walt escorted Jolene back to the table, where Ron was standing, clapping.

"My goodness!   I'm out of breath!" Jolene said, taking her seat, looking flushed and happy.   "Walt, you even make me look good.   Thank you.   I hope I didn't step on your feet too many times."

"Not at all, Jolene.   Thank *you*," Walt demurred. "You're a beautiful dancer.   You should dance more often."

The young girl Jolene had seen dancing earlier came up to the table.   "Grandpa, what's gotten into you tonight?" she laughed, hugging him around the neck from the rear. "You're burning up the dance floor!"

"Just 'cause there's snow on the roof don't mean the fire's gone out in the basement, young lady!"   Walt laughed as he patted her arm.   "You young crumb-snatchers didn't invent dancing, you know."

"Jolene, this is my daughter, Kesia," Ron said.   "Kiwi, this is Mrs. Jefferies from Channel Seven."

Kesia didn't resemble Ron as much as did LaSalles. *She must look more like her mother,* Jolene mused.   *If she does, Ron's wife must have been truly beautiful.   But she has Ron's wonderful eyes, though.*

"Hello, Kesia," Jolene offered her hand.   "It's nice to meet you."

"It's nice to meet you, too," Kesia replied, shaking hands. "I've seen you on TV a million times.   It's great that you're doing a story on my father.   Did you bring your camera man?" she asked, looking around.

Before Jolene could answer, they were joined by an attractive young woman leading Zayna by the hand.   "Here's your grandmother, honey," the woman told the child.

Zayna ran to Jolene.   "Gee-Gee, can I go to the playground with the kids?"

"What playground, Zee?" Jolene wanted to know.

"We fed the children first, so they wouldn't get antsy," the woman said.   "Now a few of us mothers are taking them to Jackson Park for a while.   It's just around the corner." The woman saw Jolene's enquiring glance.   "Oh, excuse me for not introducing myself.   I've seen you so many times on

TV that..." The woman gave a merry laugh. "Well, anyway, I'm Mona Talent, Ron's secretary."

"Actually, Mona is the *entire* office staff," Ron told Jolene with a wry grin.

"Hi, Mona. It's so nice of you to offer to take Zayna along, but..."

"Oh, please, Gee-Gee!" Zayna put in. "Erika and all the other kids are going!"

"Erika is my daughter," Mona explained. "It seems she and Zayna have already become life-long friends. Bebe and a lot of the other mothers are going. They'll be plenty of adults to chaperone. We'll take good care of her."

"Please, Gee-Gee?" Zayna entreated.

"Well, if you're sure it won't be any trouble..." Jolene began.

"No trouble at all," Mona assured her. "And this way you can finish your work with Ron on the story while we're gone."

"We've finished the story, Mona," Ron said, putting his arm across the back of Jolene's chair. "Jolene's here tonight as my guest."

Kesia looked up sharply.

"Oh. Oh, I see," Mona said, looking at Jolene in a totally different light.

Habiba stopped by the table with several kids in tow. "Come on, Mona. These hellions are getting restless." She turned to Jolene, "Is Zayna going with us?"

"Yes," Jolene said. "I just was telling Mona how nice it was of you to..."

"Good. I'm sure Zayna will have a ball." Habiba looked at Ron and Jolene knowingly, "And it will give you two a chance to get better acquainted."

A perceptive look flashed across Mona's face as she looked from Ron to Jolene and back again. "Well, guess we better get going," she said with a smile.

Jolene turned to Zayna, "Now you be a good girl, and stay with the other children.   Don't you wander off.   And mind Erika's mother and the other ladies."

"I will, Gee-Gee!" Zayna promised, as another child, presumably Erika, called out, "Zayna!   Mama!   Come on! They're ready to go!"

Mona turned to follow Zayna, who was already running toward Erika.

"We'll be back in an hour or so," Habiba said, as she too turned to leave.   "Don't worry about Zayna," she threw over her shoulder as she departed.   "You two just concentrate on having a good time!   Especially,   *you*, my workaholic brother!"   With this parting shot, she was gone.

"Come and get it before I throw it to the hogs!" a loud voice bellowed.   It was Ernie, over at the grill.

"Ready to eat, Jolene?" Ron asked.

"Yes, Ron.   The smell of those ribs has me salivating!"

Kesia rolled her eyes and sucked her teeth.   "Maybe *you* better have the chicken."   She gave Jolene a sweeping glance from head to toe.   "Pork has a lot of calories, you know."

Ron drew his breath in sharply.   "Kesia Marie Jamison! You..."

Jolene stopped him with a gentle hand on his arm. "You're right, Kesia," Jolene said smoothly.   "I probably should have the chicken."   Jolene smiled at the teenager, "But I haven't had a good plate of ribs in ages, so tonight I'm going to splurge."

"Jolene, I'm sor..." Ron began again.

"Ummm, smells delicious," Jolene interrupted.   "Ron, would you mind getting me some?"

"Well, ah, sure, Lene," Ron said, rising.   He gave Kesia a piercing "you-better-behave-yourself-young-lady" look as he left.

"I should have told Daddy to bring me some, too," Kesia said to nobody in particular as soon as Ron was out of earshot.   "Since I don't have a *weight problem*, I can afford to have as much as I want."   She tossed a challenging glance in Jolene's direction.

Jolene was at loss for words this time but felt she had to make some reply.   "Weight has a way of creeping up on you, Kesia," she said as calmly as she could.   "Believe it or not, I was slimmer than you are when I was your age.   It's never too early to start watching what you eat."

Kesia just sniffed. "Not very good at taking your own advice, are you?" she bluntly asserted.

Child or no, Jolene figured this had gone far enough. She looked Kesia dead in the eye.   "That may be true, Kesia, but there are worse things than being too heavy..."   Jolene leaned forward slightly, "Being rude, for instance."

Kesia was clearly taken aback.   She started to reply, but then glanced over at her grandfather, who so far had not said a word.   Something about the look on his face made Kesia change her mind about continuing the conversation. "Excuse me," she said abruptly, pushing away from the table and rapidly stalking off.

Walt looked at Jolene, "You know what's bothering her, don't you?" he asked quietly.

"No, Walt," Jolene said with a shake of her head.   "I honestly don't have a clue.   She seemed perfectly friendly when she first came over.   What did I do wrong?"

Walt chuckled sadly, "Not a durn thing.   But Kesia didn't know you were Akron's *date* when she first came over."

"Oh.   I see," Jolene said, although she really didn't.

Walt moved his chair a little closer.   "You see, Jolene, Kesia took losing her mother very hard.   We've had any number of problems with her.   Her school work has suffered, and for a while, she kept getting into fights.   She seems to have outgrown that, but not this thing she has about her father.   I think she feels since she's lost one parent, she has to hang on that much tighter to the one she has left. And she can't bear the thought of anyone taking her mother's place."

"Oh," Jolene said softly.   This time she really did see.

"Not that any of that excuses her behavior.   I was about to step in..."   Walt grinned, "Until I saw you were perfectly capable of handling the situation yourself."

Jolene grinned back.   "You're a wise man, Walt.   I see where Ron gets it."   She paused a moment.   "The poor kid. I remember when my son was a teenager.   It's hard enough to go through those years without all this as well."

Just then Ron came back with two food-laden plates. "Where's Kiwi?   I got these for the ladies."

"She went off on her own, son," Walt told him.

Ron set a plate before Jolene.   "Then you take the other one, Dad.   I'll go back for mine."

"No, Akron."   Walt stood.   "I think I'll go over and see what your Uncle Willie is up to.   You take that one.   You two young folks go ahead and enjoy yourselves."

As Walt walked away, Jolene smiled.   "That's the first time the term 'young folks' has been used to include *me* in a long, long time."

Ron laughed, then looked solemn.   "Lene, I've got to apologize for Kesia.   She..."

"No apology needed, Ron.   We had a little chat after you left, and we understand each other perfectly."

"Really?"   Ron brightened.   "You mean she stopped acting so...so hateful?"

"No," Jolene said, picking up a tasty looking bone and taking a nibble.   "Actually, she started acting even worse.

But still, we understand each other.   I understand that she doesn't like me, and she understands that I'm going to continue to like *her* in spite of it."

Ron just sat for a moment just looking at Jolene. "Lene," he finally whispered, "you're one in a million."

Jolene gave Ron a flirtatious side-long glance.   "Well, *I've* always thought so," she quipped.

As they were finishing the meal, Marvin Gaye's "Let's get It On" began to play.   "Come on, Lene," Ron said, taking Jolene's hand.   "I wanna show you that the older generation of Jamison men aren't the only ones in this family who know how to dance."

Jolene laughed, and let him lead her to the dance floor. But she stopped laughing as he embraced her.   Her carefully cherished memory of the tender strength of his arms didn't come close to the impact of the real thing.   She felt her body melting into his.   Ron held her even closer and sighed. "That's better," he whispered.   He looked down into her eyes.   "You felt so good the first time I held you, I couldn't wait to do it again."

Jolene's heart was beating so fast she felt breathless. For her reply, she just put her head down on his shoulder. The crisp freshness of his shirt and his light spicy cologne were intoxicating.

At the song's end, Jolene and Ron slowly stepped apart. "Whew!   A couple ought to get engaged after a dance like that," Jolene joked in a whisper, attempting to hide the quivering she felt inside.

Ron didn't smile in return.   "That's not a bad idea," he whispered in return, his eyes never leaving Jolene's.   When they finally turned to leave the dance floor, they were startled to find everyone had stopped to watch.   The crowd burst out in applause and whistles.

"You go, Ron!" hollered one guy.   "Owww!" shouted

another.   LaSalles stood off to one side and gave his father a big thumbs up.   LaSalles had his arm over the shoulder of the pretty young girl standing next to him.   And the two of them were very obviously not alone.   The girl was in the late stages of pregnancy.

"Jolene, let's grab a couple of beers, and find a little privacy," Ron said with self-consciousness due to the ovation.

"I'm with you.   Lead the way," Jolene heartily agreed. They stopped by the cooler, Jolene opting for a Pepsi instead of a beer, and headed off into the wooded area behind Ron's house.

The sun was just starting to go down, casting long shadows from the abundant trees.   "Watch your step," Ron cautioned.   "The ground's a little uneven in spots."   His hands were big enough to hold both cans in one, while he took Jolene's hand with the other.

"Ron, was that LaSalles fiancée with him just now?" Jolene asked softly.

"Yes," Ron said.   "And she's just as sweet as they come.   That knucklehead son of mine is lucky to have her." Ron looked over at Jolene.   "Shandra been living with us since school let out for the summer.   When they found out she was pregnant, her folks wouldn't let her come home. They don't even call to see if she's all right."

Jolene was scandalized.   "What kind of people are they?   How could treat their own child that way?"

"They're good people, Lene.   Really.   They're just hurt and angry.   In time they'll come around."   He paused for a moment.   "I wish the kids had waited.   God knows I've talked to Les about being careful.   But…Well, anyway, they're both good kids and they love each other and…"   Ron gave Jolene an intense look.   "I don't know how you feel about this sort of thing, Jolene, but…"

"Ron, if living has taught me anything it's taught me not to judge." Jolene's voice dropped to a whisper. "There's not a soul on this earth that hasn't done something that wasn't wise, wasn't...right. I just wish them Godspeed and all the happiness in the world."

Ron didn't speak; he just gently squeezed the hand he was holding.

They walked along in silence, until Jolene exclaimed, "Mercy, Ron! Just how big is your property, anyway?" looking out into the expanse of greenery before them.

"Actually, we just crossed over my property line," Ron chuckled. "This space is public land. It's actually the back of the park the kids went to. Nobody around here has their back yards fenced in back, to take advantage of it. Hey," he said suddenly, "there's a real live babbling brook nearby. Want to see it?"

"I never met a brook I didn't like," Jolene giggled. "Which way?"

They forged on hand in hand for another five minutes or so. Jolene was content just savoring the peace and serenity of the spot. Even the blare of the music was muffled, muted by the crickets' song. She glanced up at Ron's profile as they went along, and silently sighed, her fingers unconsciously tightening on his.

"Here we are." They had reached a clearing. There sat a very worn park bench. "Don't tell anybody, but I hauled that bench over here from the main part of the park," Ron said in a conspiratorial whisper.

And there was the brook.

"Well, that's a brook, all right," Jolene said with a grin. "But I'd hardly call it 'babbling.' I think gurgling might be a better description." The "brook" was all of a foot and a half wide, and about that much deep. There was water flowing through it, though just barely.

Ron laughed.   "It's all about quality, Mrs. Jeffries, not quantity."   He easily stepped over the narrow rivulet and stood with one foot on each side, hands on his hips.   "Bet I'm the only man you know who can span a river in a single bound."

"Uh-huh," Jolene replied.   "But a word of advice, Super Ron—don't quit your day job."

Ron came rapidly toward her and lifted her in his arms as he had the day they met.   "Allow me to carry you across the deluge, M'lady."   He stepped across the tiny channel to the bench.

"Ron," Jolene murmured, her arms around Ron's neck, "I think I could have managed to get across by myself."

"Think so?" Ron whispered, still cradling Jolene in his arms.

"Yep.   And you know what else I think?" Jolene went on, snuggling closer.

Ron sank down to the bench, Jolene perched on his lap. "Pray tell."

"I think you just wanted to take me in your arms again. At least, I hope you did..."   Jolene's voice could barely be heard now.   She looked up into Ron's eyes.   "Because I wanted you to."

Ron's lips found hers gently, tenderly.   His lips were so soft, so full.   She felt his arms tighten around her waist as the kiss intensified.   His tongue eagerly sought hers in a delicious caress. Jolene's arms circled Ron's shoulders as she clung to him, letting the incredible feeling course through her.   One of Ron's hands left her waist and began to delicately stroke her thigh.   Jolene faintly moaned at the fire his touch ignited in her loins.

Then he abruptly stopped.

"Lene, I...I think you better get up now, honey," he gasped.

Jolene jumped up, instantly contrite.   "Oh, Ron, I'm so sorry.   I should have realized I'm too heavy to sit on your lap."

"What?" Ron said, still panting.   Then he chuckled, and reached for her hand, gently pulling her down to sit next to him.   "You're not too heavy, sugar.   That's not why I wanted you to get off my lap."

Jolene looked at Ron's abashed face in puzzlement for a beat, then caught on to his meaning, "Oh."

And they both burst out laughing.

"Well, I didn't want to disgrace myself," Ron shrugged. "After all, I'm just a man."   He tenderly cupped Jolene's face.   "And you're one hell of a woman."   Once again he claimed her lips.   The fading sun cast an otherworldly light all about them.   Jolene felt as though she had stepped into a fantasy. When they finally broke apart, they just sat nestled together, Ron with his arm around her, Jolene with her head on his shoulder.

"Hey," Ron patted the abundant mass of hair atop Jolene's head.   "Is this all you?"

"Yep.   I've never cut it, except for trimming split ends."

"I knew it was real.   We men can usually tell, you know."

Jolene gently poked him in the ribs with an elbow. "Right.   You guys may *think* you can.   If you knew it was real, why did you ask?"

"Just wanted to get it on the record."   Ron buried his face in Jolene's hair.   "Damn, it's beautiful!   Most women don't want to bother with long hair these days."

"Well, my mother used to always say a woman's hair is her 'crown and glory'.   I'm not sure, but I think it's in the Bible.   Anyway," Jolene laughed softly, "I save a fortune on hairdressers."

"You do it yourself?"

"Sure.   What's to do?   I wash it when I need to, let it dry, and pin it up."

Ron couldn't seem to keep his hands off the luxuriant strands.   "Do you ever take it down?"

"Just when I go to bed."

After a long while, Ron said softly, "Hear it?   It's not very big, but you *can* actually hear the water flowing.   It's a really peaceful sound.   I come out here a lot to think. When something's gotten on my last nerve, coming here puts things back in perspective.   That's why I carted this bench over here.   This is my special place."   He leaned forward and softly kissed Jolene's forehead.   "That's why I wanted to share it with you."   Jolene just snuggled closer to him, her and squeezing the hand that was holding hers.

They sat there in silence, watching the setting sun. They didn't need to speak.   Their hearts spoke for them.

When it was almost dark, Jolene stirred.   "Ron, much as I hate to go, we'd better be getting back.   Zayna should be back from the park by now."

"Guess you're right," Ron reluctantly agreed, standing, and pulling Jolene up with him.

"Thank you for sharing this with me, Ron," Jolene whispered.   I can see why you love it.   It truly is a magical spot."

"No.   Before now it was just a *wonderful* spot."   He raised Jolene's hand, looking intently into her eyes.   "There was no magic here..."   He lifted her hand to his lips "...until you came."

Ron took Jolene into his arms for one last lingering kiss. "Okay," Ron pronounced, "much as I hate to, let's go."   And he scooped Jolene up into his arms once again.

"Ron, you're a crazy man," Jolene laughed.   "What do you think you're doing?"

"Carrying you back across the moat, my Queen," Ron

said with great import, stepping over it.   "We have just inaugurated a tradition.   Henceforth, whenever we come here, I shall carry you across."

"Oh, Ron," Jolene caressed his cheek.   "I told you that you were the strangest man I ever met."   She kissed him lightly.   "But I like it."

Ron slowly put Jolene down and leaned across the stream to pick up the cans that had fallen into it.   "We never did get to these, did we, Lene?"

"No, you were too busy," Jolene teased, taking his hand again as they started back.

"Well, you helped," Ron told her.

After a few moments, Jolene said, "Ron...nobody's ever called me 'Lene' before."

"No?"

"Uh-uh.   Most people who don't call me JJ just call me 'Jo.'

"I tried that, but it just doesn't fit.   Joe is a man's name..." his hand left hers as he put his arm around her waist. "And there ain't *nothing* mannish about you."   When Jolene didn't reply, Ron asked, "You don't *mind* me calling you Lene, do you?"

"No, it's not so much that I mind, Ron, it's just that...that..."

"That...what?"

"Well, *look* at me," Jolene finally said.   "I mean...well, Ron, I'm *not* exactly lean, you know?"

Ron stopped and faced Jolene.   "Are you upset about that smart-ass remark Kiwi made earlier?   Honey, she didn't mean..."

"No, Ron.   I'm not upset about that.   She's just a hurt, confused child.   I know she wasn't lashing out at me personally, but at what I represent."   Jolene looked down at the ground.   "But in case you haven't noticed, Mr. Jamison,

I'm what the large size catalogs euphemistically refer to as a 'big girl.' "

"You're not any kind of a girl.   You're a woman.   A real woman.   The kind of woman I thought I'd never find again."

"Was...was your wife a large woman, too?" Jolene asked softly, almost afraid to hear the answer.

"Size nine from the day I met her 'til the day she died," Ron said bluntly.   He turned Jolene to face him, and lifted her chin, forcing her to look into his eyes.

"We might as well have this out here and now, Jolene. I don't care for you either because of your size or in spite of it.   I care for *you*.   The woman—the person—inside that body.   You've knocked me off me feet from the day I met you."

Ron wrapped Jolene up in his arms, "But I sure don't mind that you're also one of the most beautiful, sexiest women I've ever seen."   Ron kissed her passionately. "Woman, you have true beauty.   And you'd be beautiful whether you weighed 100 pounds or 300 pounds.   Don't you know that?"

Jolene looked up and saw the devoted honesty of his gaze.   "I used to know it.   I had forgotten," she whispered.

"Okay.   So tell you what."   Ron was wearing his devilish grin again.   "You don't like Lene, and I don't like Jo, so why don't I call you Lena?   I've always thought Lena Horne was one of the most beautiful women on the planet..." He leaned forward, and planted a kiss on the tip of Jolene's nose, "And if that doesn't describe you, I don't know what does."

Jolene threw her arms around Ron's neck, holding him close.   "Mr. Jamison, as of tonight, I give you full permission to call me anything you like!"

CHAPTER 3

"Hi, baby."

"Hello, Ron.   Where are you, honey?"

"Just got home."

"So late?"

"Yeah.   Even after all the time you've put in helping me get it together, this grant proposal is driving me batty. Those bureaucrats want to know everything down to what color pantyhose your great-grandmother wore on her wedding night!"

"Uh, I don't think they had pantyhose back then, honey."

Ron had to laugh.   "That's my baby.   You always know how to reel me back when I get out there in the ozone layer.   Did Zee get off all right?"

"Yes.   Anna and her husband came by for her this afternoon."

"I'm going to miss that Munchkin."

"Me, too.   I miss her already.   But she'll be back in a couple of weeks.   It's only fair that her other grandparents have some time with her too.   And Zayna's going to love going to Disney World with them."

"Look, Lena, I know it's later than we planned..." Ron's voice dropped to a whisper, "but are we still on for tonight?"

To her great surprise, Jolene found herself blushing. "Yes, Ron, of course.   But you must be tired, having to work so late.   Maybe you'd rather wait until tomorrow."

"Do *you* want to wait until tomorrow?" Ron asked straightforwardly.

Jolene took a deep breath.   "No."

Even through the phone, Jolene could hear Ron release the breath he had been holding.   "I'll be there in half an hour."

" 'Kay," Jolene said softly.   She slowly put the phone

back in the holder.   Then she stood and glanced around the living room for the umpteenth time.   She rushed over to the sofa, and needlessly fluffed the pillows one more time.

Going into the dining room, Jolene checked the table again.   The silverware at Ron's place setting didn't look quite even.   She straightened it, carefully aligning the fork and spoon with the knife on the other side.   She stood back and contemplated the long candles in their elegant holders. No, that was too much.   What could she have been thinking?   Jolene hastily removed the candles and holders and put them back into the china cabinet.

She sniffed the air.   Oh, no!   Was the roast burning? Had she forgotten to turn down the oven temperature when it turned out Ron would be late?   Jolene ran to the oven.   No, everything here was just fine.   She opened the oven, and basted the roast yet again, although it showed no signs of drying out.

Going back to the dining room, Jolene again contemplated the table.   She went back into the kitchen, and retrieved the candles and holders, and returned them to their former places.

Slowly Jolene turned and entered her bedroom.   The twenty-five watt pink bulb she'd placed in her bedside lamp filled the room with a soft rosy glow.   The candle under the potpourri pot wafted the delicate scent through the air.   Her brand new Martha Stewart sheets lay in crisp display enveloping the queen sized bed. *Well, I've certainly got the right bed,* Jolene thought for some obscure reason.   *I'm queen-sized—it is, too.*

She glanced into her bathroom.   Yes, she'd remembered to put out extra towels, and a fresh toothbrush.   Okay, time for the final check.

Jolene went to her vanity and studied herself in the mirror.   Why had she decided to wear this dress?   Red, of all colors!   She started for the closet but stopped herself. *Oh, no you don't, girlfriend.   You've changed three times already.   You look fabulous in this dress.   And red is your best color.*

Jolene sank down on the bed.   *Time to get a grip, Jolene.   You're a mature woman in her late-forties.   You're a grandmother for heaven's sake, not some school girl waiting for her first date.*   But it had been so long since her last date—*this* kind of date—that it may as well have been the first.

And what if this is not what Ron...expected?   After all, they hadn't really *said* that tonight would be the night.   But with children in the house for both of them, it was like having built-in chaperons.   And it had been understood that neither felt comfortable with...intimacy with the children there.   All they'd really *talked* about was Ron coming over for dinner. But with Zayna away, she knew they'd both thought that tonight...

Jolene knew Ron respected her, truly cared for her.   But what would he think if they...if she allowed him to...   Zane's father—she had thought *he* cared for her, too.

Woman, wake up, Jolene scolded herself.   *This is the twenty-first century, not the nineteenth.   You can't even turn on the TV without seeing people twisted up in every position imaginable—and that's just on the* network *channels!*

Yes, but that was TV.   Since she was a TV personality, no one knew the difference better than Jolene.   This was real life.   Over the past month, her relationship with Ron had become very precious to her.   Almost...indispensable.

She looked up into the mirror.   A lock of her hair had come undone again.   She quickly pinned it up and picked up the brush to smooth it.   Just then the doorbell rang.   Jolene was coiled so tightly she jumped and dropped the brush. *Okay, okay, calm down.   This isn't some stranger.   This is*

Ron.   This is your man.

Jolene picked up the brush, placed it back on the dresser, and went to the door.   The doorbell rang again just as she reached it.

"Hi. Ron."

"Hi.   I was beginning to think you'd run off with the milkman."

Jolene laughed nervously.   "There aren't any milkmen anymore, Ron."

"Oh.   Right."

Something was wrong.   Normally that would have gotten a laugh out of Ron.   Jolene suddenly realized he was still standing there on the porch.   "Well...ah..."   Jolene jerkily swept her arm aside, gesturing for him to come in.

"Oh.   Excuse me," Ron said quickly, rushing in so fast he bumped into Jolene.   "Oh.   Sorry."

"No problem.   Ah...won't you have a seat?"

"Oh.   Thanks."   Jolene started to follow Ron into the living room, when he stopped and turned so suddenly he bumped into her again.   "Oh.   You all right?"   Before she could answer, he thrust forward the bottle of wine he was carrying, almost pushing it into her abdomen.   "This is for dinner."

"Oh.   Thanks."   Jolene took the bottle.

"And these are for you."   Ron held the bouquet of roses up so high they brushed Jolene's nose.

Jolene sneezed.   "Thank you.   They're lovely.   I'll go put them in water.   Why don't you pour the wine?"

When Jolene returned with the roses in a vase, Ron was standing awkwardly in the middle of the living room floor. "Uh...Can...may I have a corkscrew?"

"Oh.   Of course."   Jolene went to the kitchen and returned with the corkscrew and two glasses.   "Forgot the glasses, too," she said.

It took Ron three tries to get the corkscrew inserted. And then he couldn't pull out the cork.

"Maybe running it under warm water?" Jolene suggested.

"No, I've got it.   It's coming, it's com..." The cork came out of the bottle with a loud *pop*.   Ron was tugging on the corkscrew so hard the neck of the bottle slammed against his chest, spilling wine all over the front of his spotless white shirt.

"Oh.   Damn.   And this is a new shirt, too."   Ron looked down at himself in confusion, as if wondering how he had gotten himself into such a predicament.   "Did any get on the carpet?" he asked, looking down at the floor around him as he set the bottle down on an end table.

"No.   I don't think so.   Don't worry.   It's Scotch-Guarded.   Let me get you a towel."   Jolene went into the kitchen for the third time in almost that many minutes.   She came back into the living room so quickly she stubbed her toe, lost her balance, and came crashing forward into Ron. The two of them fell together on the sofa in a heap.

They looked at each other for a second in total shock, then simultaneously burst out laughing.   They laughed until they were both on the floor with tears running down their cheeks.

"Hoo, boy!   What the hell was *that* all about?" Ron said, wiping the tears from his face.

"Well..." Jolene could hardly catch her breath.   "I don't know about you, friend, but I was acting that way because I was scared spitless."

"Really?"   Ron took her hand.   "You weren't really *afraid* of me, were you, Jolene?" he asked with great concern.

"No, Ron.   Not afraid of *you*.   Afraid of...   Well, maybe afraid isn't the right word.   Anxious.   I guess anxious is the word.   Ron...it's just that it's been so long..."

"Yeah.   For me, too."

"Really?   How long?"

"Since well before I lost Marie.   She was so weak and…"   Ron just shrugged and gave Jolene a little sad smile.   He paused a moment before asking, "You?"

"You want to know the truth?"

 Ron nodded.

"The truth is…so long that… I can't really remember when it was.   That long."

Ron didn't speak for such an extended time that Jolene grew anxious all over again.   When he finally did speak, she jumped.   "Jolene, do *you* want to know the truth?"

She slowly nodded.

"The truth is that…I love you. I love you with all my heart.   I thought I'd never feel this way again.   I want you so badly I ache, but I want things to be right between us.   I want you to feel comfortable with me.   I want you to be sure.   So I'll wait.   I'll wait as long as it takes.   Until you're sure you love me, too."   Ron took both Jolene's hands in his, his heart in his eyes.   "Because I love you that much, my beautiful Lena."

Jolene slowly slid her hands from his grasp, and rose to her knees.   She lifted her right hand and removed the one large clip that held her hair in place.   It fell in a rushing black torrent, down her shoulders, down her back, past her hips, past her knees, until the ends lay in a black satin stream upon the carpet.   "I told you there's only one time I take down my hair.   When I'm going to bed.   I love you, Akron Jamison."

Ron stood and took both Jolene's hands once again to help her to her feet.   Hand in hand they went into Jolene's bedroom.   Ron looked about him.   "This room looks like you."   He turned to Jolene and took her into his arms, but then he pulled back slightly and looked into her face with concern.   "Baby, you're trembling."

Jolene looked up at him with a shaky smile, "Don't look now, fella, but you are, too."

Ron looked startled, and then a slow grin crossed his face, "Yeah.   Guess I am."

"I hope we're vibrating on the same frequency," Jolene teased, unbuttoning his shirt.

"Something tells me we are," Ron replied, unzipping Jolene's dress.   The dress fell in a puddle at her feet.   She was left clad in only the red lace bra and panties she had so carefully selected just for this special evening.

Ron gasped, and stepped back, staring.   He slowly sank down to sit on the bed but didn't move another muscle.

"Ron?   Ron, what is it?" Jolene breathed.

"Oh, my God," Ron huskily replied.   "Lena.   You are *so* beautiful.   You're like a goddess.   Come here, baby."

Jolene came slowly forward until she was standing between his open thighs.   She reached out and pulled the open shirt down his arms.   He wore nothing beneath, and the powerful muscles of his massive chest and arms glistened with the sheen of the sweat now lightly covering them.

Ron reached behind Jolene and unfastened the slender clasp of her bra.   The bra fell away, revealing her lush, full breasts, their dark brown nipples plump and crinkled in anticipation.   Ron cupped Jolene's right breast, lightly squeezing as he took the swollen nipple into his mouth. Jolene moaned at the ecstasy of his hot, wet tongue as it flicked back and forth across her nipple.

Ron's hands slipped down to her buttocks, and he pulled her tightly against his body.   Jolene could feel the hard throbbing of his manhood against her quivering thighs.   Ron slowly stood, and Jolene reached between them, undoing his belt and pants, and unzipped his fly.   She sank to her knees as she slowly pulled the trousers down.   Standing once again, her hand snaked beneath the fabric of his shorts until it found its target.   Ron groaned from deep in his chest.   His lips descended on hers, his tongue greedily exploring hers. Then Ron put his arms around her waist, and they rolled onto the bed together, Jolene's hair loosely wound around them both, as they floated off into ecstasy.

Jolene slowly returned to consciousness.   Her senses of touch, sound, and smell were immediately activated: the house smelled of roast, the telephone was ringing off the hook, and Ron had his arm across her waist.   She decided to deal with them in priority.   She leaned over and lightly kissed Ron's lips.   He smiled, murmured something intelligible, and snuggled even closer.   *This man of mine is one sound sleeper,* Jolene thought, a fragile smile touching her lips.   *But then, he has good reason to sleep soundly just now.*   The now surely overdone roast could wait.   *Who could be calling at this hour of the night?*   Marveling that the still ringing telephone hadn't awakened Ron as well, Jolene picked it up, "Hello?"

"I need to speak to my Dad," came the terse reply.

Still groggy, Jolene shook her head.   "What?"

"I *said* I need to speak to my Dad."   It was Kesia.

"Kesia?"

"Yes?"

"What's the matter, honey?   Is there an emergency?"

"Look, Jolene, that's for my father and me to discuss.   I didn't call to talk to *you.*   I want to talk to my father.   And don't try to pretend he isn't there.   I know he is.   Where else would he be in the middle of the night?"

Jolene had to struggle to stay calm.   "I never said he wasn't here, Kesia."

"Then can I speak to him...*please?*"   It wasn't the word. It was the way Kesia said it.   It was about the rudest "please" Jolene had ever heard.

Holding her temper in check, Jolene simply replied, "Hold on."   She turned to Ron, who miraculously was still asleep.   "Ron?"   Jolene lightly shook his shoulder.   "Ron? Honey, wake up."

Ron finally stirred.   He opened his eyes and seeing Jolene, his face broke out in a sleepy grin as he stretched his arms, and flexed those strapping shoulders.   "What is it, insatiable woman?"   Jolene quickly put her hand over the telephone's mouthpiece.   "What are you trying to do, girl, cripple me?" Ron continued, pulling Jolene's face down to his, kissing her.

"Ron, Kesia's on the phone, honey," Jolene finally managed to get out.

Ron became instantly alert.   "*Kesia?*   What time is it?"

Jolene checked the bedside clock.   "It's four-thirty."

"Oh, my God.   Something must be wrong."   Ron took the telephone from Jolene.   "Kesia?   This is Dad, honey. What's the matter?"   As he listened, the transformation in Ron's appearance and demeanor was terrible to see.   First, he became flushed, his chocolate complexion initially taking on a ruddy tinge which became so pronounced he actually turned a shade darker.   He almost seemed to swell, his lips cramped in an angry scowl.

After listening for a bit, he finally said into the phone, "Kesia, I'm only going to say this once.   Get off this phone, and go back to bed.   We'll talk when I get home."

Ron listened for another moment. "When am I coming home?   You'll know when I get there."   Ron hung up.

"Ron?   What's wrong?   Is she all right?" Jolene asked anxiously.

Ron flopped back on the pillow, just looking disgustedly

at the ceiling.   "What's wrong is that I have a daughter who seems to have forgotten which of us is the child and which of us is the parent."

"I don't understand."

Ron rose on one elbow to face Jolene, "She woke up to go to the bathroom, and noticed that I wasn't in my room."

"And?"

"And nothing.   That's it.   She found out I wasn't home, so she took it upon herself to call over here."

"But...why?"

Ron put his arms around Jolene and pulled her next to him.   "That, my love, is the question.   Why?   Why is she making a career out of getting into trouble at school?   Why doesn't she want to go on with her life?   Why does she resent you so much?   And most importantly, what can I do to help her?"

Jolene paused a moment before she spoke, "Ron, we know the answer to the 'why' questions.   She still hasn't recovered from her mother's death.   And she's afraid of losing you."

"I know, Lena.   When Marie died, it hurt all three of us."   His voice dropped to a whisper, "Hell, for a while I thought I was going insane.   But the last thing Marie would have wanted was for us to die with her.   Les has moved on, and found love."   Ron hugged Jolene tighter and kissed her forehead.   "And thank God, now I have, too.   But I don't know how to reach Kesia."

Ron's eyes were tortured as he looked at Jolene.   "She's my baby, Lena.   My little girl.   Pain in the butt that she can be sometimes, I love her."   A tear slowly slid down his cheek.   "And I don't know how to help her."

Jolene leaned over and kissed the tear away.   "We'll find a way, Ron.   Somehow, we'll find a way."

"Lena, I know this is hard on you, too, baby.   Please

hold on. Please don't give up on us. We'll *have* to find a way." Ron kissed Jolene tenderly. "Because now that I've found you, I couldn't bear to lose you."

Now tears came to *Jolene's* eyes, as she embraced him. "Lose *me*? Mister, there's no way you're *ever* getting rid of me."

"Jolene? Jolene, may I see you for a moment?" Keith Mays stood in his office door.

"Keith, Frank and I are on our way to cover the demolition of the Block Building. Can it wait until I get back?"

"No. No, I'm afraid it can't. I'll call the newsroom and have Jennifer go with Frank to cover the story."

Jennifer Paxton was the fluffy blonde Keith had brought with him when he reported as the new station manager six months before. And Jolene was already ticked about Keith's repeated attempts to further Jennifer's career at the expense of her own.

"That's *my* story, Keith. I've already done all the background work. Jennifer doesn't know a damn thing about it. You can't send her."

"Jolene, you forget who runs this station. I decide who covers what. Now, please." He turned sideways and gestured for Jolene to precede him into the office.

Jolene eyed him silently for a moment. "All right, Keith. Maybe it *is* time we had a talk." She went into his office and took the chair in front of his desk.

Keith closed the door behind him and sat down at his desk. He picked up the phone and made the call to the newsroom. Then he turned to Jolene. "I just received a call from Vince DeMarco. He's the CEO of DeMarco

Construction."

"I know who he is," Jolene replied.

"Then you also know his company is our biggest advertiser."

"Yes, I know that, too. What does that have to do with me?"

"Mr. DeMarco wanted to know why this station is taking a political stand with one of his business rivals."

"Keith, I haven't the faintest idea what you're talking about."

Keith leaned forward. "All right, let me spell it out for you. I'm talking about your affiliation with H.O.M.E. Construction."

Jolene stared him dead in the eye. "I don't *have* an affiliation with H.O.M.E. Construction."

"Jolene, now please." *Every time he calls me 'Jolene' it grates on my nerves. Why does he just refuse to call me JJ, like everybody else around here?* "Everybody at the station knows you've been...ah, seeing Akron Jamison," Keith was continuing.

Jolene crossed her arms. "Keith, who I'm 'seeing,' as you put it, is quite frankly none of your business."

Keith turned red. "It is when it affects the reputation of this station."

Jolene leaned back in her chair and crossed her legs. "Oh, really? How so?"

"Don't play games with me, Jolene. Akron Jamison is one of the owners of H.O.M.E. Construction."

"Yes, he is. And although—as I've already said—it's none of your business, I will tell you openly that I'm in love with Akron Jamison. But my relationship is with *him*, not his company."

"Can you deny that H.O.M.E. Construction has a bid in for the next housing renovation grant?"

"No, I don't deny it.   Why should I?"

"You helped prepare that proposal, I believe?"

"Yes, I did.   I was a journalism major.   I'm good with words, both spoken and written.   What of it?"

"And you're scheduled to speak before the city council in support of that proposal?"

"Yes.   And your point is?"

"My point is this station's policy.   This station does not openly support any political cause unless it is expressly voted on and approved by the Board of Directors."

Jolene's mouth flew open in shock.   "Keith, you can't be serious!   I've done nothing to violate that policy.   That policy pertains to partisan elections and issues on the ballot, not a matter of this nature.   And the actions I took were as Jolene Jeffries, private citizen, not as an agent of the station."

"Really?   What about the interview with Jamison a few weeks ago?   Didn't *that* involve the station?"

Jolene sat back in her chair, "The company didn't even decide to *bid* for the grant until after the interview was completed.   That interview had nothing whatsoever to do with the grant proposal."

"The Board may see the matter differently, Jolene.   I plan to put the matter before them."

Jolene stiffly stood.   "You go right ahead and do that, Keith.   I have nothing to hide.   I've been at this station nine years.   I'll stand on my reputation.   Now, if you'll excuse me."   Jolene turned to leave.

"One minute, Jolene.   There's another matter we need to discuss."

Jolene turned.   "Yes?"

"I've been reviewing some of the tapes of your past work.   You're really quite an excellent reporter."

"Yes. I am."

"But I couldn't help but notice you've changed

considerably since you started here," Keith smirked, looking Jolene up and down. "To put it bluntly, you must have gained a good thirty pounds since you first started here."

Jolene was thunderstruck at his audacity.

"As you know, Jolene," Keith went on, "ours is a visual medium. And I'm concerned that your current appearance may not be of the…ah, professional standards we expect."

Jolene's eyes narrowed dangerously. "No, Keith. That's not what you're concerned about. You're concerned about putting that Barbie doll you brought with you in my place. That's what all this foolishness about policy is about, isn't it? And since I'm an excellent reporter, as you so accurately pointed out, you know I'd sue the station for every cent it's got if you tried to get rid of me just because you've decided I'm not cute enough for you."

Keith shot up from his desk. "How dare you!"

"How dare I? Well, I'll tell you, Keith. I dare like this—if you make one move in any way to unfairly hamper my career, I'll lay a lawsuit on this station, and on you, *personally* such as the world has never seen. How's *that* for a dare?"

Keith slowly sat back down.

"Thought you could dig it," Jolene threw over her shoulder as she turned once again.

"Jolene. One last thing."

Jolene turned once again. "Who do you think you are, Columbo?"

Keith gave her a look of fabricated regret. "Jolene, I was sincerely hoping it wouldn't come to this." He opened a desk drawer and pulled out a manila folder. "I've been doing some background work on my own, checking out the information in your personnel file. You went to college in Georgia, didn't you?" He browsed through the papers in the file and looked up at Jolene with a malevolent grin.

"Amazing what a detailed review of college records can reveal."

Jolene slowly sank back down to her seat.

Jolene looked at her watch as she pulled her car into Ron's driveway.   She hoped Ron would be there soon. When she'd called him at the site, he said he'd get here as soon as he could.

I should have told him before now, Jolene chided herself. *I love this man.   How could I keep this from him?*   But she knew why.   She didn't want to lose Ron.   To lose his respect, to lose his love.   *But you can't build a life on a lie, girl.   You should know that by now.   Did you really think no one would ever find out?   And now that you've finally found the love of your life, that lie could destroy everything.*

Jolene looked at her watch again.   What could be keeping Ron?   He knew she'd never call him like this in the middle of the day unless it was urgent.

She went to the front door, she rang the doorbell.   Les was working with Ron, and Kesia was in school, but Shandra, who only worked part-time, might be there.   If she was, Jolene didn't want to startle her.   Jolene rang the bell several times, but there was no answer.

Jolene suddenly remembered Ron showing her the location of a hidden key, under a phony rock in the front yard.   Kesia was always losing her house key, and Ron kept one there so she wouldn't be stuck one day with no way to get in.   Jolene had been there one evening, working on the grant proposal, when Ron had to replace the hidden key.

Jolene retrieved the key from its hiding place.   After looking once last time to see if Ron was approaching, Jolene let herself in.

"Hello? Hello?" she called, on the off chance someone was there and had not heard the doorbell. There was no answer.

The smell hit her a moment later. Marijuana. She'd never used it but could certainly recognize the unmistakable scent.

Ron's not going to like this one bit, she thought. *I know Les is young, but he ought to know his father don't play that, especially in his house.* Les was always running errands to get building materials and such. *He must have come by here on a break,* Jolene's thoughts ran on. *Or maybe it was Shandra. I hope she's not messing with that stuff while she's pregnant.*

Jolene looked around the house. Ron had painstakingly restored all the fine features of the old house; the beautiful hardwood floors, the graceful stairway, the high, beamed ceilings. But much as she loved the house, Jolene had difficulty seeing herself there. *I'd always feel like an intruder here after all the years Ron spent here with Marie. I don't think I could ever feel that I was the mistress of this house.* Jolene laughed bitterly at her own foolishness. *At this moment, it's questionable as to if the man will even want to ever see you again, after today. And here you are imagining yourself as his wife?*

Jolene went into the kitchen in the back of the house to wait for Ron. She decided to make a pot of coffee since Ron drank the stuff all day long. As she was putting the water in the coffee maker the second smell hit her. Smoke. Jolene looked at the stove. No, all the burners and the oven were off. Anyway, the smell didn't seem to be coming from in there.

Jolene ran frantically through the lower rooms of the house, desperately looking for the source of the smell that was becoming stronger by the second. Upstairs. It must be coming from upstairs.   She ran to the foot of the stairway.   Yes, the smoke was visible here, drifting down from above.   Just then a piercing screech began.   A smoke detector.   Jolene ran quickly up the stairs.   Thick black smoke was pouring from Kesia's room.   Even from several feet away, Jolene's eyes began to water, and she began to cough.

Putting the scarf she wore around her neck over her mouth and nose, Jolene went into the room, hoping the fire was small enough for her to put out alone.   The drapes all along one wall of the room were aflame, and the fire had spread to the walls and the dresser.   The smoke was so thick it was difficult to see, but just as she was turning to run back out, she faintly made out a form lying motionless on the bed.

"Kesia!   Kesia!"   Jolene ran to the bed, and shook the girl, calling her name over and over.   Kesia groaned but did not move.   Too late, Jolene realized she should have called the fire department before she came upstairs.   She snatched up the phone on Kesia's bedside table.   It was dead.   Jolene glanced down.   The cord connecting the phone to the wall was melted through.

She dashed into Ron's room.   This phone was cordless, and thank God, it was working.   Jolene quickly called 911 and reported the fire.   Then she darted back to Kesia.

The fire had spread even farther, the smoke thicker than ever.   Jolene was beginning to gasp for breath through the coughing that racked her body.   Jolene knew Kesia was too heavy for her to carry.   Somehow, she had to wake her. Jolene ran to a window and flung it open.   Instantly the room was clearer as the fresh air poured in.   Jolene then bolted into the bathroom.   Glancing desperately around her, she snatched up the wastebasket, dumped its contents on the floor, and quickly filled it with water.

She ran back to Kesia.   The fresh air had dissipated

much of the smoke, but it had also fueled the fire.   The flames leaped even higher than before and were spreading throughout the room.   Jolene was beginning to feel woozy but managed the dash the container of water into Kesia's face. The girl jerked violently and began to cough, but her eyes did not open.

"Kesia!   Kesia!   You have to wake up!" Jolene shouted, shaking Kesia once more.   "Do you hear me? You've *got* to wake up!"   Jolene drew back her hand and slapped Kesia across the face as hard as she could.

Kesia's eyes flew open, as her arms flew out, flailing out at Jolene.   "Lemme 'lone.   I'm sleepy," she murmured groggily.

Jolene could hear fire sirens in the distance.   *But I can't leave her here.   I won't leave her here.   They may not get here in time!*

"No!   You have to get up!   We've got to get out of here!" Jolene screamed.   She slapped the girl once again.

"No! Lemme alone!" Kesia said, but this time sat up.

Jolene crouched and pulled Kesia's arm around her neck. As the girl's arm raked across her head, Jolene's hair came loose and fell tumbling down her back.   Ignoring it, Jolene tightly grasped Kesia's hand, on her shoulder, and stood, pulling the girl up with her.   Jolene put her other arm around Kesia's waist.   "Walk, Kesia!   I can't carry you!   You have to help me!"

Kesia sluggishly moved one foot forward.   "That's it, honey!   You can do it!" Jolene encouraged her.

"Jolene!   Jolene!   Where are you?"   It was Ron.

"Oh, thank God!" Jolene breathed.   "Ron!   Ron, we're up here!"   Jolene was trying her best to shout, but her voice only came out in gasps.   Then Ron appeared in the doorway.

"Jolene!   *Kiwi!*   Oh, my God!"

"Help me, Ron!   We've got to get her out of here!"

Jolene screamed.

Ron grabbed Kesia and threw her over his shoulder as though she was weightless.   "I've got her, Lena!   Let's go!"

Jolene suddenly felt intense heat at her back. "Ron! I'm on fire!"   Jolene's hair was ablaze. She twirled in terror, only causing the flames to spread.

"Stop, Jolene!   Stand still!   You're only making it worse, baby!"   Ron dumped Kesia back on the bed and grabbed Jolene in a bear hug.   He and flung Jolene and himself to the floor, rolling with her, beating the flames with his hands until they were extinguished.

Ron quickly helped Jolene to her feet, "It's out now. Are you all right?   Did you get burned, baby?"

"I...I'm not sure, but I'm okay.   But, oh, Ron! Look at you!" Both Ron's hands were scorched, and already blisters were beginning to appear.   But Ron was already bending to pick up Kesia.

A fireman suddenly appeared at the doorway.   "It's all right, folks!   This way!"   Another fireman grabbed Kesia and dashed with her out of the room.   Ron picked up Jolene and carried her down the stairs and through the door as other firemen rushed in with hoses.

Outside, Kesia was on a gurney, and paramedics were holding an oxygen mask over her face.

"Let me take over here, buddy," a paramedic said to Ron, looking at Jolene, who was coughing and gasping for air.   The paramedic had another oxygen mask in his hand for her.

"It's okay, honey.   I'm all right."   Jolene gasped out. "Go see to Kesia."

"I'll be right back, baby," Ron said, seeing that Jolene was in good hands.   Ron rushed forward.   A policeman stopped him.   "Just hold on, sir.   Everything's under control."

"You don't understand! She's my daughter!" Ron cried, as he rushed past the policeman.

One of the paramedics working on Kesia turned. "It's all right, sir. She's got a bad case of smoke inhalation, but she wasn't burned. She should be fine; she's even conscious now. Come on, you can talk to her."

Ron ran to Kesia's side. "Daddy, oh, Daddy, I'm so sorry! I skipped school today. I...I had some weed. It made me sleepy, so I laid down, and...Oh, Daddy!"

"It's okay. It's okay, baby girl. You're all right. That's all that matters right now."

Jolene appeared at Ron's side. "Ron, is she okay?"

"They said she'll be fine, honey. How about you?"

"I'm okay. Just a minor burn on my back."

"We need to get your daughter to the hospital now, sir. It's just precautionary," the paramedic told Ron.

"Then I'm going with her," Ron said.

"I guess you are," the guy replied, looking down at Ron's hands. "Those burns need to be treated."

They wheeled Kesia's gurney to the waiting ambulance, with Ron and Jolene trailing alongside. "Don't worry, honey," Ron told Kesia. "I'm coming with you."

Kesia put out her hand and grasped Ron's arm. "Daddy, I want Jolene to come, too."

"I'm right here, Kesia," Jolene smiled down at her, taking her hand.

"Oh, Jolene! After I've been so hateful to you, you risked your life for me! Can you ever forgive me?" Kesia looked up at the charred and uneven strands of Jolene's hair. "And your hair! Your beautiful hair!"

Jolene's smile grew even wider. "It'll grow back. I look at it as a pretty good trade—I lost a hairdo, but gained a friend."

"Well, we're quite a pair, Mr. Jamison," Jolene said that evening.   "You with your bandaged hands and me with my bandaged back."   They were sitting at Jolene's kitchen table, having dinner.

"And I'd say we were pretty lucky, considering," Ron replied.   "We should both be able to go back to work in a few days.   And they told me Kesia will be released tomorrow.   They just want to observe her overnight.   Even the damage to the house was mostly confined to that one room.   Thank God I'm insured to the max.   And thank God you were there!   When I think what could have happened if you weren't!   That reminds me.   What was it you wanted to talk to me about this afternoon?"

Jolene's smile faded.   "Ron, some things are going to come out soon.   Things about me.   Things you need to know."

Ron placed one of his bandaged hands over hers. "Well, what is it, baby?   You know you can tell me anything."

"Ron, this is something I should have told you before. I'm so sorry I didn't."

Ron looked worried now.   "What is it, Lena?   Are you sick?   Are you in some kind of trouble?"

Jolene rose from the table and walked a few paces away. She abruptly turned to face Ron.   "No, I'm not in trouble… now.   But I was.   I *was* in trouble my senior year of college."

"Honey, I'm not following you.   What are you trying to tell me?"   Ron rose and went to Jolene.   "Look, here, girl. You're the woman I love.   Whatever your troubles, they are *my* troubles, too.   Now, whatever it is, just tell me."

Jolene looked down at her hands, "Ron, I'm Jolene

Jefferies, but I'm not *Mrs.* Jefferies. She looked up at Ron, her eyes brimmed with tears. "Ron, I've never been married."

Ron blinked quickly. "What?"

"I've never been married. Zane's father was one of my college professors. I thought he loved me. And he didn't tell me he was married until I told him I was pregnant." Jolene laughed bitterly, "I was the only graduate with a baby under her robe. After Zane was born, I moved to another city, stuck 'Mrs.' in front of my name, and told everybody I was divorced.

"I had to tell you now because it's going to come out at the grant hearing. My new station manager found out about me. He said he'd use the lie I've been living all these years to discredit me if I testified. DeMarco Construction is afraid of you beating them out for that grant. And Keith is afraid they'll pull their advertising from the station if you do.

"I should have told you before. It shouldn't have taken this for me to tell you. But I was ashamed. I didn't want you to lose respect for me."

Ron didn't speak for a long moment. "You don't have to go to the hearing, Jolene. I'd understand," he finally said.

"No, Ron. What you're doing is too important. And anyway, I'll be damned if I let Keith hold that over my head to control me. The only way to stop a blackmailer is to let the secret he's manipulating go public.

"I'm going to call Zane tonight to tell him. I don't want him to hear it through the grapevine. I think he'll take the news okay…at least I hope he will." Jolene looked down at the floor. "But I had to tell you first."

Ron moved a step closer. "I see. So you've never been married?"

Jolene shook her head sadly.

Ron put a finger under her chin and lifted her face. His

eyes were shining as they gazed lovingly into hers. "Well…would you like to be?"

"You may now kiss the bride!"

LaSalles bent to lift the veil from Shandra's face.

Jolene looked up at Ron and squeezed his hand. "You're not losing a son.   You're gaining a daughter— Gramps."   Jolene smiled over at Shandra's mother, who was cradling infant Akron Jamison the second in her arms.

The guests all applauded as the newlyweds embraced, but instead of starting up the aisle with his bride LaSalles held up his hands for attention.

"What in the world?" Ron wondered.

"Ladies and gentlemen," LaSalles began, "Shandra and I thank you for being here with us on this special day.   But we were not the only engaged couple to enter this church this afternoon."

"Huh?" Jolene said.

"As most of you know," LaSalles was continuing, "my Dad and his lady are planning to be married next week in a small ceremony at home.   We tried to talk them into making this a double wedding, but they insisted this be *our* day.

"But what they didn't know is that we, their children, insist they be married in church, so...Mr. Jamison and Ms. Jeffries—would you please step forward?"

"But...but, son," Ron stammered, "I don't even have the wedding rings here!"

Zane stepped forward, "Oh, yes, you do—Dad."   He reached into his pocket and pulled out a small black velvet box.   "Although we had a devil of a time sneaking them out of your room."

"So *this* is why you and Marlena got leave so early, you

rapscallion!" Jolene scolded her son.

"Who better to give you away, Mama?" Zane grinned at Jolene as Marlena came forward to kiss her mother-in-law's cheek.

Zane looked down and handed the velvet box to Zayna. "Here you go, baby.   Ready to be the ring bearer as well as flower girl this time?"

"Yes, Daddy."   Zayna looked up at Jolene, "Come on, Gee-Gee.   It's time for you and Papa Ron to get hitched."

"Here's your bouquet, Jolene."   Kesia handed Jolene a huge bouquet of red roses.   The two just stood looking at each other a moment, then Kesia impulsively threw her arms around Jolene.   "Oh, Jolene," Kesia said, drawing away, "I'm sorry!   I mussed your hair!"   She stroked Jolene's new chin-length bob, brushing the displaced strands back into place.

Jolene just leaned forward and gently kissed Kesia's cheek.   "What's a mussed hairdo," she whispered softly, "...between friends?"

"I have your marriage license right here," LaSalles patted his breast pocket.

With tears in her eyes, Jolene looked up at Ron.   "Well, looks like we're outnumbered.   What do you say, Chief?"

"I've already asked you to marry me, darlin'," Ron kissed Jolene tenderly.   He looked deeply into her eyes, "But, honey, will you marry me—right here, right now?"

Jolene beamed as she put her arm through his.   "Jolene Jeffries Jamison is the most beautiful name in the world.   I don't want to wait another week.   Do you?"

Ron lifted her hand to his lips.   "No.   So, let's go jump that broom...Triple J."

EPILOGUE

"Grandpa!   Grandpa, wake up!"

"Huh?   What time is it?   What is it, princess?"   Ron groggily asked.

"It's eight-thirty.   And you promised to take me to my dance lesson today," Zayna declared.

"Zayna," Jolene put in, having herself been awakened by her granddaughter's persistence, "your lesson isn't until eleven o'clock.   Why are you waking your grandfather and I up at the crack of dawn on a Saturday?"

"I don't want to be late, Gee-Gee," Zayna insisted.

"Be that as it may, young lady," Jolene continued, "your timing leaves a bit to be desired.   Now you march..."

Suddenly a baby began to cry in the next room.   "Now you've done it, girlfriend," Jolene scolded.   "You woke your brother!"

"I'll get him, Gee-Gee!"   Zayna bustled from the room with all the big-sisterly importance her budding twelve-year-old body could muster.

Ron rolled over to take Jolene into his arms.   "Good morning, Mrs. Jamison."   He kissed her tenderly.   "Have I told you I love you today?"

"No, I don't believe you have, sir," Jolene murmured, snuggling deeper into his embrace.

"Now, you know my favorite way of saying I love you doesn't need words, don't you, baby?" Ron ran his fingers through Jolene's hair, tenderly winding it's copious length around his hand to gently pull her face to his.   His lips captured hers once again as they slowly sank back into the still warm, delicious depths of the pillows.

"Gee-Gee!   Zayna won't let me play with Zak!" Eight-year-old Akron Jamison the second burst into the room, and with a flying leap, jumped into the bed between

Ron and Jolene.

"*Ooof!*" Ron gasped as his grandson's poorly aimed lunge planted a small foot squarely into his stomach. "Now, look here, A.J.," Ron told the child, "Haven't I told you a hundred times to knock before you come in?"

"I'm sorry, Grandpa." The boy threw his arms around Jolene, "Good morning, Gee-Gee."

"Good morning, honey," Jolene kissed him. "Now what's all this about Zayna not..."

"He's just mad because I told him Zak couldn't have that Hershey bar he tried to give him," Zayna said, striding back into the room with ten-month-old Zak on her hip.

"And what were *you* doing with a Hershey bar, young man?" Ron challenged the boy, tussling with him in the bed. "Have you been plundering in the kitchen cabinets without permission again?"

A shamefaced A.J. was spared having to come up with a reply when Zak took a deep breath and began crying again with a vengeance.

"Uh-oh. I think it's time for somebody's bottle," Jolene surmised.

"Yes, I was just going downstairs to get it," Zayna asserted.

A.J. put his head on Jolene's shoulder, and looked up at her with beseeching eyes, "Gee-Gee, will you make me some bald eggs this morning?"

"That's *boiled* eggs, A.J.—honestly!" Zayna rolled her eyes at her cousin, full of proper pre-teen disdain at such baby talk.

"*You* used to call them 'bald' eggs, too, when you were little, honey," Jolene gently chided.

"She did?" A.J. asked with glee. "Bald eggs, bald eggs, Zayna Ann likes bald eggs!" he taunted her.

"My name is Zayna *Jo*Anne, boy. If you're going to

say it, get it right."

"Okay, Zayna...*Ann*," A. J. came back.

"Look," Ron said, "I can see nobody's getting any more sleep this morning, so why don't we all go downstairs. *I'll* cook breakfast this morning."

Breakfast was clearly still the subject topmost on Zak's "to do" list. He stopped crying, looked his sister in the eye, and stated in a no-nonsense tone, "Bah-Do."

"Okay, big man," Zayna laughed. "I get the message. One 'bah-do' coming right up. Come on, A.J. I'll turn the TV on for you, and you can look at cartoons while I feed the baby."

Ron and Jolene rose to don their robes as the children went downstairs. "You know, honey," Ron said, "I'm happy our kids have gotten so tight they go out together. But there's only one drawback—we get to babysit three grandchildren all at one time!"

"Don't even try it, Akron Jamison! You light up like a firefly whenever the kids are here, and you know it."

"Yeah, I guess I do," Ron admitted with a chuckle. "It's great having Zane and Marlena close by, now that they're stationed here."

"Yes, it is, honey," Jolene agreed, tying her robe, and sitting at the vanity to brush her hair. "And the four of them work so hard, I'm glad they like to get with Les and Shandra for a night on the town every once in a while." She paused with the brush hovering over her head in mid-stroke, gazing dreamily out the window at the beautiful flowers surrounding the yard.

Ron came up behind, and put both hands on her shoulders, "What is it, baby?"

Jolene sighed. "I was just thinking that right out there, on that very spot, was where we first met, when this house was just a shell. I would never have dreamed that I'd be living in this house one day."   She reached up to put one hand over Ron's, and looked into the vanity mirror, smiling at Ron tenderly.   "Living here—with you."

"I called this place my dream house.   But it never would have been..." Ron leaned forward and pulled Jolene up from the vanity bench and into his arms, "...without you." Just then the doorbell rang.

"Gee-Gee?   Grandpa?   Somebody's at the door!" Zayna superfluously called up the stairs.

"Be right down, honey!" Ron called.   He kissed Jolene one last time.   "I love having the kids here, but..." he held Jolene a little tighter, patting her behind, "I miss how we *usually* spend our Saturday mornings."

"Behave yourself!"   Jolene laughed up at him.   "We don't want to scandalize the children, frisky Papa.   And anyway..." she squeezed Ron's buns with a devilish wink, "there's always Saturday *night!*"

As they made their way downstairs, a baby started to cry.   And then another baby began to cry.   And then another.   "Uh-oh," Ron told Jolene.   "You know what that means."

Sure enough, when they entered the kitchen there stood Kesia, with one of her twins in each arm.

"Hello, darling," Jolene said, going to Kesia, and kissing her cheek.   Jolene took one of the twins, while Ron took the other.

"What's the matter with Gee-Gee's big girl?" Jolene cooed to the baby, who stopped crying to give her a big toothless grin.

"Hi, Mom.   They're cranky because I bundled them up and ran out the house with them while they were still half-asleep."   Kesia looked at Jolene pleadingly.   "I hate to ask you, but my babysitter is sick, and I have an important seminar downtown in half an hour.   This *would* have to happen when their father is away on a business trip. Would you mind watching them for a couple of hours?"

"Of course not, honey." Jolene sat at the kitchen table, bouncing the baby on her knee. "You go on to your meeting. We'll be just fine."

"Thanks, Mom," Kesia said, giving Jolene a kiss. "You're an angel. You, too, Daddy." Kesia kissed Ron on the cheek as she made for the door. "I'll be back by one. Oh, and Daddy, don't forget you promised to speak to my fifth-grade class next Wednesday." She flashed Ron a bright smile. "We're studying architecture, and I promised them the world's best architect would come and tell them how it's done!"

"I'll be there, baby," Ron promised. "I have a meeting with the mayor that morning on the grant renewal, but I saved the afternoon for you. My intrepid customer relations manager highlighted it on my calendar." He looked at Jolene, "Right?"

"Yes, sir, Mr. Jamison," Jolene assured him. "I most certainly did."

A somewhat frenzied hour or so later, the three babies were taking a nap, A.J. was deep into a video game, and Zayna was practicing for her dance class.

Jolene rested her head on Ron's shoulder as they gently rocked on the back porch glider. Ron leaned over to kiss her forehead. "Penny for your thoughts, beautiful Lena," he whispered, putting his arm around her shoulders.

"I was just saying a little prayer. Saying thank you, for my children, for my grandchildren, for my home, and for my heart."

"For your heart? Woman, what are you talking about?"

"I'm talking about *you*—my love, my heart." She looked up into Ron's eyes. "And you know what they say..." Jolene caressed her husband's cheek. "Home is where the heart is."

OTHER BOOKS BY RAYNETTA MANEES

All For Love
(The SuperStar Series: Book One)
Available in digital and paperback
formats

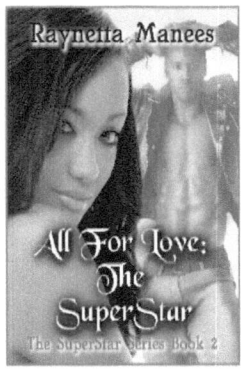

All For Love: The SuperStar
(The SuperStar Series: Book Two)
Available in digital and paperback
formats

Fantasy
Available in digital and paperback
formats

Wishing On A Star
Available in digital and paperback
formats

Follow Your Heart
Available in digital and paperback
formats

My Alzheimer's Diary
Available in digital and paperback
formats

Classic Paperback Books

All For Love
released September 1996, ISBN 0-7860-0309-X
rated 5 stars on both Amazon and B&N

Wishing On A Star
released August 1997, ISBN 0-7860-0423-1
rated 4 ½ stars Amazon   5 stars B&N

Follow Your Heart
released September 1998 ISBN 0-7860-0560-2
rated 5 stars on both Amazon and B&N

Fantasy
released August 1999 ISBN 1-58314-030-1
rated 5 stars on both Amazon and B&N

Heart Of The Matter
Heart of the Matter, released January 2002 ISBN 1-58314-262-2
rated 5 stars Amazon   Not yet rated on B&N

A Mother's Touch
A three author anthology containing Raynetta Manees'
novella, "All The Way Home"
released May 1999 ISBN 1-58314-015-8
Rated 5 stars on both Amazon and B&N

ABOUT THE AUTHOR

Raynetta Manees is a best-selling, award-winning author. Her books are in both digital and print editions and she is traditionally published and self-published. She's done it all! She has written several five-star Black romance novels as well as a non-fiction book about #Alzheimer's. All Raynetta's books are on Amazon and B&N.

Her landmark first-person novel, **All For Love**, first released in 1996, is now considered a Black romance classic. An updated e-book edition of the novel was released in 2013. This book is now Book One of *The SuperStar Series*.

September 2016 marked Raynetta's 20th anniversary as an author. She celebrated this milestone with the release of Book Two of *The SuperStar Series*, **All For Love: The Superstar** in Sept 2016. The book is a finalist for the 2017 Emma Award for the Best Contemporary Romance of the year. The Emma is the premier award for black authors of romance.

Raynetta is the very first recipient of the Award of Excellence from RomanceInColor.com for her novel **Follow Your Heart.**

She is currently working on Book Three of *The SuperStar Series*, **All For Love: The Superstar's Daughter**, which will be released in 2018.

Raynetta's author page on Amazon.com is www.amazon.com/author/raynettamanees

All of Raynetta's books are rated four/five stars by readers on Amazon.com and BN.com (Barnes and Noble).

Raynetta Manees is a graduate of Wayne State University, with a degree in Mass Communications. She retired as a Federal government executive administrator after a 28-year career. Raynetta now writes full-time. Her love of the media arts is reflected in her novels, whose characters are involved in some aspect of entertainment/media.

Raynetta has been a solo vocalist since childhood. Her stage name is "Rayne," and her first CD, "Singing in the Rayne," a collection of smooth jazz vocals, was released in December 2012.

The author is an accomplished actress who has appeared in numerous stage productions and in TV and radio commercials. As an on-air radio personality, she was known as "Shalimar Brown, the baddest girl in town" on AM 1180 WXLA.

Raynetta stepped away from her career as a notable romance novelist in June 2015 to pen her first non-fiction work, **My Alzheimer's Diary.** The book explores Alzheimer's effect on her family and her own journey of diagnosis.

Raynetta welcomes your comments at her website www.RManees.com. She can also be reached via email at RManees@aol.com (Please show "Reader" and your name in the subject line.)

You may also reach Raynetta via:
Facebook: Raynetta Manees, Author
Twitter: @raynettaman,
Pinterest: Raynetta Manees Author on Pinterest
Instagram: ms.manees
Mail: P.O. Box 3203, Southfield, MI 48037
Goodreads Author Page:
goodreads.com/author/show/21931.Raynetta_Manees